Escape to Danger

Escape to Danger

Roy Nichols

Escape to Danger

© Roy Nichols 2018

The story and locations are a fictionalized account of events recorded in the Book of Acts, Chapters 27 and 28. Except for biblical characters and locations mentioned in those chapters, all other characters and locations in the story are the product of the author's imagination. Any resemblance to actual events or places or persons, living or dead, is entirely coincidental.

Published by
Lighthouse Christian Publishing
SAN 257-4330
5531 Dufferin Drive
Savage, Minnesota, 55378
United States of America

www.lighthousechristianpublishing.com

Chapter 1

"Get up, you ungrateful pig!" Before Timon's eyes could adjust to the half dark of the slave quarters, Cassius, the slave master, jerked him from his sleeping mat and shook him as a hound shakes a catch. "I'll teach you to steal from a good master." A gloved fist crashed into Timon's jaw and sent him sprawling across the hard-packed dirt floor.

"Enough, Cassius. If you kill him we'll never find the pearls. Give them to me, Timon." Marcellos, Timon's owner, extended his hand. "Did you really think you could steal from me and not get caught? You've betrayed my trust."

As Timon struggled to his feet, his surprise gave way to rage. Though he was only eighteen years of age, he stood eye to eye with his master and surveyed him coldly before speaking. "I'm not a thief. I have taken nothing from you." Though his voice was calm, clinched fists and the ripple of restrained muscles betrayed his furry. "The last time I saw the pearls was when you showed them to Governor Vitellius for his approval. That was aboard ship before we sailed from Rome. I saw you place them in the travel pouch you wear around your neck. You said you would take them to the silversmith to be made into the earrings he ordered when we arrived back here in Myra."

"I told you he knew where you kept them. He's the one I saw creeping out of your quarters just before dawn," Cassius lied. "There's no mistaking him. He still walks like one trained for the games. He has yet to learn humility."

"I have treated you well," Marcellos continued, ignoring Cassius. "I know your background, your knowledge of mathematics, writing and languages. I have trusted you and allowed you to accompany me to the market place. I've taken you on my trips abroad. I have treated you like a son. One day I would have freed you. Why would you betray my trust?"

"Master, I have not. Though I hate the bonds of slavery, I have honored your position. I am not a thief. I have stolen nothing from you."

"Do you dare to call me a liar?" Cassius shouted as he once again slammed his fist into Timon's bloody face.

When consciousness returned, Timon found himself bound to a post in the center of the compound. His body was pulled taut, wrists tied together above his head and secured to the whipping stake.

"Do you know what it means to be flogged?" Marcellos asked.

"Yes, master." Timon shuddered as he imagined the lashes slicing through skin and muscle.

"You are young and have been a good slave. I don't want you to suffer this. Tell me where you've hidden the pearls. You'll be punished for the theft, but I promise you, Cassius will not touch you with the lash." Timon shook strands of black, sweat-dampened hair from his face and glared at his accuser. Pride edged his voice.

"You know I am not a thief. I have never taken even the smallest coin that belonged to you. I can't give you what I do not have. No beating can change that. Why don't you ask Cassius..."

The whip exploded, tearing flesh and blood from Timon's back and a scream of agony from his throat.

Cassius licked his lips in anticipation as he poised the whip for the second stroke. Marcellos began the long count. Again and again the lashes ripped Timon's flesh. At last, drained of strength and pride, Timon's legs gave way beneath him. Only the thongs biting into his wrists supported his weight. Confused images roamed his mind. In the swirling mists of agony, a sunny patio in Ephesus opened before him. His father was chained between two Roman soldiers. Then memories of the chaos of the slave markets swirled through his brain. He remembered being sold at auction like an animal. In a moment of reality, the sweaty, hate filled face of Cassius formed and faded. At last Timon's tortured body embraced the oblivion of unconsciousness.

"Enough, Cassius."

"But you haven't finished the full count."

"What good is it to beat an unconscious man. He can tell us nothing. If he had anything to tell, the whip would have loosened his tongue by now. Alexos, you are quartered with him. Cut him down and see to his back."

From the doorway of the slave quarters stepped a man, frail with age, his bald head ringed with short white hair. Deftly he unfastened the restraining thongs and gently lowered Timon to the ground. The old man's eyes filled with tears. He shook his head and muttered to himself. "It is well your father's dead. Seeing you like this would break his heart. But I am here to take care of you. Perhaps that's why the gods allowed me to be sold into this house with you."

Hours later Timon awoke to the pungent smell of vinegar and olive oil. He gasped in agony as his old tutor carefully sponged blood from his back. "Be still, brave one. I must clean these cuts or they will not heal."

"Alexos, I didn't steal those pearls. Marcellos had no right to have me whipped. He had no right…"

"Have you been a slave these many months and learned nothing? It is you who has no rights. You must forget the first sixteen years of your life in your father's house. You are no longer the son of a rich citizen, just as I am no longer the tutor of that citizen's children. The moment the governor had your father arrested and confiscated his estates, you know that part of your life ended forever. When Marcellos bought you, you became a slave, just as I am. You are a piece of property. You have no rights. He can do with you as he pleases."

"But I didn't steal the pearls. I am not a thief, I tell you."

"Of that I have no doubt. You grew up in a noble house. I did not tutor you through the years of your childhood to make a thief of you. Cassius stole the pearls. I watched him slip from the master's house in the dark hours before dawn."

"And you let me be beaten for it? Timon tried to rise from his mat as his voice rose in indignation. "Why didn't you tell Marcellos?"

"Do you think it would have made a difference? Cassius hid the pearls before he accused you. He is a free Roman. I am a Greek slave. My word is nothing against his.

"But why would he accuse me?"

"You have much to learn, young one. Haven't you noticed his growing hatred for you? Once, the master depended on him. He even traveled with him while trading in the agora or on his buying trips abroad. But since Marcellos discovered your skills, it has been you, not Cassius who accompanied him. You, a slave and a Greek, have won the master's favor and taken Cassius' place. If he can discredit you, his position will again be secure. Beware of him. He will kill you if you give him an excuse."

"I might as well be dead. If Marcellos thinks I am a thief, he will sell me to some warship as a galley slave. I'd rather be dead than spend my life chained to an oar."

"Do not be so eager to die. Marcellos will not sell so valuable a property. Even now he begins to doubt that you took the pearls. You must rest. You have paid the price for the pearls. One day they will be yours. Accept your fate. You can't fight against the will of the gods. Sleep now. Tomorrow you are expected back at work."

As the old man shuffled down the corridor, Timon's grim face softened. He recalled his childhood and the many times his tutor had comforted him and given him advice. "No, old friend, I will not accept my fate. I will find a way to change the will of the gods. I will escape my fate."

In the weeks that followed, Timon's back healed, but his anger grew like a festering wound. He was not allowed to work in the offices at the dock but was kept confined to the main house which stood on a high cliff overlooking the Andracus River.

From his office in the villa, Marcellos ran his merchant shipping empire, buying grain in Egypt and selling it by the ship load to the markets in Rome. He profited, not only from the price of the grain he sold to feed the hungry mobs of Rome, but also from the fees he charged for the use of his cargo vessels. In his warehouses, along the docks two miles below the city, he kept ships' stores and supplies from which he provisioned both his own fleet and the commissioned grain ships of Rome.

While Timon was not allowed the freedom of the docks, he helped Alexos keep the records. Under the watchful eye of Marcellos, he counted and sorted the many currencies that poured through the cash bins. At the end of the day, he balanced the accounts and prepared shipping manifests. At work, he was a silent submissive slave. At night, in the darkness of the slave quarters Alexos rubbed oil into the healing lacework of scars covering his back. Meanwhile Timon planned and dreamed dreams of freedom.

"I'm going to escape from here with the last ship of the season. Will you help me?"

"Escape? You young fool. There is no escape. This is no time for such talk. Marcellos already begins to doubt your guilt. He knows the beating you received was enough to loosen the tongue of any man. He'll soon return you to your work at the accounting tables. He needs your skills. Be patient. One day you'll gain your freedom. In the meantime . . ."

"No Alexos. There is no 'meantime.' There is only now. I will not stay the slave of any man, much less one who thinks I am a thief. Isn't it enough that my father died at the hands of a lying, cheating governor? Dad was innocent, and he died. I will not allow that to happen to me. I will escape, with or without your help."

"Wasn't that beating enough? You've seen what they do to runaway slaves. Marcellos can have you drawn and quartered. At the least, he'll brand you as a troublemaker. If you try this you may indeed end up in the galley of a warship. I know how you think, Timon.

Once an idea gets into your head, you never turn it loose. But you must give up this one. It can only bring you misery and death."

"I won't get caught. I know a way. With your help I can do it. I know I can."

"If you run away, Marcellos will be sure you took the pearls. He will never give up searching for you. His reputation with Governor Vitellius is at stake. Besides, where will you go? You can't go back to Ephesus. That's the first place he would look for you."

"Not to Ephesus. I'll go to Rome. When I was there with Marcellos, I heard about a whole section of the city made up of runaway slaves. Even the soldiers do not dare enter it without an armed force."

"Yes, slaves, but also every kind of criminal and cutthroat running from Roman law. It is a dangerous world. They will rob and kill you for a crust of bread. It is no life for a Greek."

"It is better than being a slave."

- - -

As summer wore into autumn, the prophecy of Alexos came true. Timon was once again assigned to the docks. He made a great show of his submission. Even Cassius was convinced that he had broken the young Greek's spirit. In the warehouse, inside a shipping crate, Timon stored dried foods, wine, water skins and supplies.

He and Alexos worked late on the last day of autumn. The Aries, a large grain freighter, lay anchored in the outer harbor. It was the last ship scheduled to depart for Rome before winter storms closed all shipping on the Great Sea. To complicate their work, a coastal trading ship from Adramyttium dropped anchor early in the afternoon. It had been commandeered by a Roman centurion under authority of Governor Felix for prisoner transport.

Marcellos had assigned Timon the responsibility of finding quarters for the guards and their prisoners while he negotiated with the centurion for their transport to Rome aboard the Aries. Timon watched as the chained and branded criminals filed by. He shuddered, knowing they were destined to provide entertainment for the Emperor in the coliseum in Rome.

A separate group, made up of a Macedonian, a Jew and a well-dressed young man who might have been Greek, caught Timon's attention. Julius ordered separate quarters for this small group. He seemed to give them a respect not due to common prisoners.

"Most of these poor wretches are slated for the arena," he over heard Julius explaining to Marcellos, "but this Jew, Paul, is a Roman citizen who is to stand trial before the emperor himself. I'd not like to be stuck here all winter with this lot."

"The Aries is due to sail at high tide tomorrow morning. She's ready in the outer harbor. As you can see, she's a grain ship and as slow as a sea snail but well built and big enough to handle three hundred passengers and crew. She's under command of Captain Nikkos, a seasoned sailor in these waters."

When Timon had finished marking the centurion's gear for loading aboard the Aires next morning, he pulled the large shipping crate from the warehouse, marked it with Marcellos' seal and consigned it to an agent in Rome. His task finished, he returned to the slave quarters and forced himself to eat a hearty meal. His sleep was restless.

Well before dawn he rose quietly and slipped his feet onto the cool floor. Heavy breathing and the snores of exhausted slaves masked the whisper of his bare feet as he crept toward the white rectangle of moonlight marking the exit from his quarters and his first step toward freedom. Already he could feel the chill of the predawn morning. As he pulled his cape around his shoulders, a pair of rough hands locked over his mouth and around his throat.

"Even if you refuse my warnings and advice, you can't leave without telling your old teacher farewell." Alexos whispered in his ear. Timon nearly collapsed as his old tutor released his grip. When he started to speak Alexos interrupted. "Tell me nothing. Then I will be unable to betray you should Marcellos or Cassius question me. Quickly. Give me your cape and take this one. It will keep you warm and may one day buy your freedom. Guard it well." The old man held Timon at arm's length for a moment memorizing his proud, young face. Tears filled the old mans eyes as he visualized better days when he tutored the lad on a warm porch in Ephesus. Wiping his eyes, he embraced Timon as if he were a son. Then Alexos turned and quietly disappeared into the dark silence of the olive grove.

Indecision swept over Timon. He realized he was seeing his old tutor for the last time in his life. The reality of his plan confronted him. Behind was the security of the familiar. Ahead lay uncertainty, fear, danger and possibly death, but also freedom. "Goodbye, old friend," he whispered His resolve strengthened, he turned toward the murmuring sounds of the Andracus River winding its way to the harbor, the unknown and freedom.

Chapter 2

Below the dock, shoulder deep in filthy water, Timon shuddered as overhead, Cassius hailed the guard. "You. On the dock there. Have you seen a tall Greek slave, with short black hair and the build of an athlete?"

Timon drew himself deeper into the muddy harbor and waited for the watchman's reply.

"No one's been around here this morning. Why do you want him?"

"He's a runaway who belongs to Marcellos. Name's Timon."

"Oh yeah, I know him. He sometimes works in the warehouse."

"That's him."

"Why would he run away? He had a good deal. A slave in a rich house like that is better off than most of us freemen. Besides, doesn't he know what they do to runaways?"

Ignoring the question, Cassius answered. "He's a thief and a troublemaker. Marcellos bought him to help in the shipping business. He's educated. You know the kind, too good to accept what the gods have decreed."

Timon burned with rage as he listened to the half-truths and lies Cassius spouted. "You filthy Roman dog," he thought. "You stole those pearls and caused all this trouble. But maybe you did me a favor. Without that beating I might never have had the courage to run away."

"If you see anything suspicious, let me know," Cassius shouted as he left the dock. "There's a big reward for his capture. I'll add one hundred denari of my own if you bring him to me personally. Keep an eye on the Aries there. He may try to slip on board. She's the last ship out of here this season. If we can keep him from getting aboard, he'll be stuck here for the winter. We'll get him eventually. You might check under the docks in case he's gotten this far. I'll be in the tavern. Send for me if you see him."

Numbing cold crept into Timon's body. Now he had a price on his head. He expected that, but why would Cassius offer his own money as a personal award? The shuffle of a guard's sandals overhead brought Timon back to his immediate problem.

A mile offshore, lost in fog, the heavily loaded Aires tugged at her double anchors as she rode the growing swells outside the silted shallow harbor. Binding his cape around his waist like a rope, Timon mentally measured the distance to the Aries. He calculated his chances for making good his escape. He was a strong swimmer but fighting the incoming tide and waves of the outer harbor would be a challenge. Behind him he heard the guard scrambling down the rocks of the retaining wall toward the water. Better to die trying than to face Cassius' whip again.

Like a marsh frog, he drove his lean body beneath the surface. With muscles hardened by training and slavery, he propelled himself toward the Aires. Soon his body was screaming for air. Allowing only his face to break the surface, he rolled onto his back and drew great gulps of the onshore breeze into his starved lungs. The wide sweep of his arms drove him through the opposing current until he reached the breakwater of the outer harbor. There the water cleared, and the waves of the open sea tossed him about like floating trash. After riding a wave to its crest, he caught sight of the carved swan's neck decorating the prow of the Aries. Though she seemed closer, a wide expanse of rough water still separated him from the ship.

The taste of fear rose, bitter in his throat, as fatigue began its torture of his legs. The cold of the October sea penetrated both muscle and bone.

Still he forced himself. From another time and place an echoing voice pushed aside his weariness and fear. "Don't fight the sea, Son. Let it carry your weight. Take slow steady strokes." Memories of sunny beaches outside Ephesus filled his thoughts. The words became a chant.

"Slow and steady. Don't fight the sea." He forced a rhythm for his aching arms until they became too heavy for his muscles to lift. Gray, salty water swirled over him. Again and again he struggled to the surface. At last he abandoned himself to the waves. The undercurrent grasped him, like a floating log, and swept him toward the open sea. He opened his eyes and saw only a towering blackness overhead. This must be what it's like to die, he thought.

Suddenly the fire of salt in open wounds restored his senses. Around him the sea was red with his own blood. He braced for the final assault of the creature that had attacked him. The next wave dragged his bleeding shoulder across the jagged edge of barnacles encrusting the hull of the Aries. In grateful agony and grinning at his fears, he pushed off from the ship and swam the few strokes to a taut anchor cable.

As he waited for his strength to rebuild, he heard raucous gulls greet a pale sun breaking through the fog. The ship would soon be visible to anyone on shore. He locked his tired legs around the cable and began his climb to the deck above.

By the time he dragged his body onto the ship, the fog was fading. There remained little time before the passengers and crew would board the ship. He oriented himself to the ship's layout. Though somewhat larger than the ships on which he had traveled with Marcellos, the Aries was a standard member of the grain fleet. Forward he saw a shadowy structure. That would be the cabin area and the entrance to the cargo hold below.

Somewhere down that passage was a half empty shipping container bearing the seal of Marcellos. Inside was dried food, wine and water skins and dry clothing. Bending low to avoid the eyes of the watch, he approached the cabin structure. When he peered around the corner he found himself looking into the face of the night watchman, slouched against the open doorway, rocked to sleep by the ship's roll. Across the harbor he could hear shouted orders as sailors made preparations for boarding.

The watchman was one of the freemen Marcellos often employed on the dock. At least he would not be sailing with the ship. But how can I get into the hold without waking him?

Unbinding his wet cape from his waist, Timon shook out its wet wrinkles and wrapped it around his shoulders. Perhaps, if the guard had other things on his mind, he would not notice its condition. Stepping in front of the sleeper, Timon grabbed the man's shoulder and shook him roughly. "Is this the way you guard my master's goods? I could have cut your throat with your own sword. Look alive, man."

Surprise and confusion swept over the guard as he scrambled to his feet, denying he had been asleep.

"I don't have time to listen to your excuses." Timon laced his voice with authority and impatience. "Marcellos sent me to inspect the cargo he consigned to his agent in Rome. Where did you have it stowed?"

"It's in the forward hold with the ship's tackle and extra sailcloth. I'll get a lamp and show you."

"Never mind. I can find it for myself. You had better make preparations for receiving the passengers. Their boat left the docks just behind me. If I ever catch you sleeping at your post again, Marcellos will hear about it."

The guard, thankful for his reprieve, hastily retreated. Trembling with relief but amused by his own bravado, Timon slipped quickly into the hold of the ship. Below decks he felt his way through the blackness of the ship's belly until he came to the tackle and cargo he sought. His lacerated shoulder throbbed with each bump of unseen obstacles in the darkness. At last he found the sealed crate he had prepared. For a moment his stiff fingers fought the binding thongs clumsily. Closing his eyes and forcing down panic, he visualized the knots he had used. Then, in the silence of the hold, he knew he was not alone.

In a distant corner he heard the click of small feet climbing over cargo. Peering into the deeper blackness he could see several sets of shining eyes. Rats. The ship was infested with them. There was no time to think about that now. Unleashing the last thong, he lifted the lid of the crate and crawled inside. Relief and exhaustion traveled in tides through muscle, brain, and bone. Opening a packet of dried fruit, he quickly chewed and swallowed washing down the welcome sweetness with stale water from a wineskin. Then he collapsed into exhausted sleep.

- - -

The increasing din of passengers and crew boarding the ship and the ache of cramped muscles woke Timon.

"Get those prisoners aboard. The Centurion wants the prisoner Paul assigned to his quarters."

"Yes, Captain Nikkos, but where shall I put the grain merchant's agent? He demands private quarters."

"Private quarters with over two hundred people on board? Cassius will share quarters with the physician and the Macedonian. Quarter them near the guards. We can't have them tramping about interfering with the working of the ship."

Timon recognized the voice of Captain Nikkos of the Aires, but had paid little attention to the orders. Inside his crate he was able to sit up by flexing his knees but was unable to stretch his cramping muscles. The pain in his shoulder seemed worse now, but at the mention of the name "Cassius," he forgot all other miseries.

Every fiber of his body shouted, "Run," but he was trapped in a cage of his own making aboard a ship with his worst enemy. He fought to gain control. He reasoned with himself. There are over two hundred people on board. I saw the passenger manifest. Surely I can keep hidden among so many. But why is Cassius here? He couldn't know that I am aboard. No. Maybe Marcellos sent him to protect his interests in Rome. Timon's mental rationalizations did little to comfort him. Regardless of the reason, Cassius was aboard. He shuddered knowing a confrontation was inevitable.

A sudden pitch of the deck slammed Timon into the side of the crate and he cried out in surprise. Touching his shoulder, his hand came away with the unmistakable warm stickiness of blood. Cassius was not his most urgent problem. Timon knew that wounds like his, left unattended, quickly become oozing sores. In spite of the risks, he must attend to his shoulder. The ship, free from the restraints of anchor cables began to pitch and roll as Captain Nikkos brought her about and steered away from the harbor and into the open sea.

The great ship rolled and struggled to gain way against the tide. Timbers groaned as helmsmen leaned on the tiller, forcing the twin rudders to bite into the northwesterly swells. He heard the clicking of small claws as rats scampered for nooks and crannies where they would ride out the coming storm. *If I don't do something about this shoulder*, he told himself, *I'll die before Cassius gets a chance to kill me. I can't disappoint the slave master.* His feeble attempt at dark humor calmed him, and he groped around the crate until he found a small bundle of clothes from which he took a worn tunic. He folded the garment and soaked it with wine. *I may starve later, but this will keep the cuts from putrefying.* Using leather lashings from the crate, he bound the makeshift poultice in place.

The pitch and yaw of the ship grew worse. Time after time, the deck tilted steeply as the vessel struggled to the crest of a wave only to shudder and plunge into the yawning trough before meeting the next wall of water.

Chapter 3

"Julius!" Captain Nikkos shouted over the wail of the wind tearing at the reefed sail on the main mast. "The wind has shifted to the north. As centurion you are in charge, but your plan to reach Cindos and run across to Cythera and ride out the storm won't work. This northerly gale will drive us aground on the north shore of Crete. We must put in at Cindos and wait for a fair wind."

"Cindos has only limited facilities. I don't want to be stuck there with this bunch of prisoners. This late in the season, the weather could keep us there until spring. What other choices do we have?"

"Very few, my friend. We could take our chances and make a run to the east around the southern tip of Crete. We might find some shelter there."

"Can your steersman hold a course for Crete?" Julius asked.

"No one can hold a course in this weather, but we can run to the east until we round the headland at Salmone. With the island between us and the gale, we should be able to track along the coast and reach the harbor at Fair Havens."

"I don't think we have any other choice, Captain. Give the orders."

As Captain Nikkos shouted the course change to the steersman, the ship shuddered beneath them.

"What was that?" Julius asked. He both felt and heard a rumbling from within the ship's hold.

"Something is loose below decks. I can't spare any men right now. Can you get some of your people to help?

How about that physician, Luke? He's been to sea before... and his friend Aristarchus too. Take Cassius with you also. He's done nothing but complain since the storm started. A few hours in the hold should give him something new to occupy his mind."

The centurion quickly drafted a crew and led the way to the hold. Below, he surveyed the chaos by the flickering lamp Cassius held. Red wine from crushed amphora mixed with olive oil. Cases of dried fruit and bundles of wool and flax hurtled from side to side as the ship yawed and pitched. "Be careful with that lamp. Drop that into the oil and we'll have more than a storm to worry about. Cassius, you have loaded cargo for Marcellos. Take two men and secure the cargo along that bulkhead. Luke, you and Aristarchus shift these crates back to Cassius so they can be secured. Throw overboard anything that has been broken, opened or damaged. I will sign the manifests noting the losses."

Julius' training and skill in Roman organization began to bring order to the hold in spite of the pitching of the ship. Loose cargo was lashed in place and broken crates and baskets removed.

"Luke, help me here," Aristarchus called. "There's something under this crate. I think it's a body. He's been crushed by the falling crates."

As the last of the heavy cases were removed, Luke knelt over the crumpled form. "He's still alive." As Luke examined the man, he gave instructions. "His legs are not broken. Straighten them, but don't move him. Some of his ribs may be broken and he's bleeding badly from that gash on his head."

As Luke carefully spread Timon's cape over him and applied pressure to the head wound, the clean-up detail gathered around, peering at the unconscious form on the deck. "He's not one of the crew." Julius said. "Do any of you recognize him?""

Aristarchus peered into the young face. "I don't think he came on board with our group. I've never seen him before."

"Well, well, well," Cassius purred. "I've caught up with him at last. This is the thief I've been chasing. He stole some valuable pearls from Marcellos and then ran away. He must have stowed away while the ship was in the harbor. Look at this." Cassius held up the seal of the House of Marcellos with which Timon had marked the crate where he had hidden food. "Let me have him. I'll tie him up in my quarters and hand him over to the authorities when we reach Fair Havens. They know how to deal with runaway slaves."

Luke's response was calm but edged with anger. "Sir, this young man cannot be moved. It would kill him. He is seriously injured and will need medical care for many days if he is to survive."

"Who cares if he survives? He's nothing but a thief and a runaway slave. And who are you to tell me what to do? You're nothing but a slave yourself…"

"Wrong, Cassius." Julius interrupted. "Luke and Aristarchus have bound themselves as slaves for this voyage so they can accompany my prisoner, Paul. He is a freeborn Roman on his way to appear before Caesar himself. Aristarchus is a Macedonian. Luke is a Greek and both are freemen. Luke is a healer, a physician. Perhaps you know him by his Roman name, Lucanus. He is well-known in the Empire. I advise you to listen to what he says."

"I don't care if he's the Emperor's grandmother." That slave belongs to me. He's the reason I came on this voyage."

"It was my understanding you were going to Rome as an agent for Marcellos. No one said anything about a manhunt."

"That's my private business and none of yours," Cassius retorted.

"As centurion, everything that happens on this ship is my business. The ship is under my authority, and so are you. Now, return to your quarters. Luke will care for the slave here in the hold. If he survives, he will be returned to Marcellos but not until I release him. In the meantime, he's Luke's responsibility, not yours."

Throughout the afternoon and the following night, Luke stayed in the hold, treating his young patient, relieved from time to time by Aristarchus. About mid-morning the following day, Timon struggled back to consciousness. "Where am I?"

"Peace, young man. You are not alone. We are aboard the Aries. You've had an accident, but you're going to survive. The pain you are feeling is from some broken ribs and a nasty cut on your head and lacerations on your back. I've treated them, and they will heal, but you must rest quietly."

"Who are you, and why are you caring for me? I can't pay you anything."

"I am Luke, a physician. I've signed on as a bond slave for this voyage so I can go to Rome with my friend, Paul of Tarsus. I don't expect to be paid to take care of you."

"Come on. Nobody does anything for nothing. By now you know I'm a runaway slave. Why do you care what happens to me?"

"One thing at a time, my impatient young friend. You're right. I'm not doing something for nothing. I'm a Christian, a follower of my Lord Jesus Christ. What I do for you, I do for Him in His name. He loves and cares for you just as he does for me. I too love and care for you. It is a debt I owe. It is a part of living in The Way."

"A Christian? I know about you. My father once heard one of your group speak. He was in Ephesus. Your man started a riot there as I remember."

Yes, that was Paul, the man I follow to Rome. This is a long story and one you're too tired to hear. What about you? How did you come to be on board the Aries? And why is Cassius so determined to get his hands on you? What did you steal?"

At the mention of the name, Cassius, Timon began to tremble. "You mean Cassius knows I'm on board? What did he tell you?"

"Yes, he knows you're on board, and he is very eager to have you arrested and turned over to the authorities as a runaway and a thief."

"He lies." I'm a runaway and with good cause. But he's the thief. He stole some pearls from Marcellos, my master, and blamed it on me. Cassius knew I didn't have the pearls, but still he nearly beat me to death because I couldn't tell Marcellos where they were."

"I find that hard to believe, Timon. Lying to cover your theft will only lead to more pain and difficulties. I think Cassius will follow you any place you go. He seems willing to kill you to get the pearls. Why don't you give the pearls to Julius, the centurion, for safekeeping.

Perhaps we can arrange for your return to Marcellos once we reach Fair Havens."

"I don't have the pearls. He's lying, I tell you. The continued pitching of the storm-tossed ship and his own rage left Timon teetering on the edge of unconsciousness. But Luke persisted.

"You do have the pearls, Timon. I found them sewn into the hem of your cape when I covered you with it." Luke thrust the thumb-sized lumps in the garment's hem into Timon's hand and closed his fingers around them. We'll talk about this again later. But consider what I've said. If Cassius finds you with the pearls, I believe he will not hesitate to kill you and return the pearls to your master to claim the reward."

Pain, fear and confusion rolled like waves over Timon as he lay in the hold of the Aries. He listened as storm driven winds hurled waves across the deck overhead. In moments of consciousness, Timon wrestled with the reality of the hard lumps in the hem of his cape. The pearls... Had he really stolen them? Was he a thief? At last, like a specter, he visualized the face of Alexos and heard his voice. "You have paid the price for the pearls. They will be yours. Take this cape. It will keep you warm and may one day buy your freedom. Guard it well."

At last the whole story was clear to him. Alexos had seen Cassius steal the pearls. He must have followed him until Cassius had hidden them. After the beating, the old man must have taken the pearls from their hiding place and sewn them into the cape. Timon's eyes filled with moisture, and a smile crept over his fear-strained face as he realized the risk the old man had taken for him.

"Well, it's good to see a smile on my patient's face. The calmer seas and a safe harbor seem to have agreed with you." Timon opened his eyes to look up into Luke's kindly face. "Have you considered my advice about the pearls?"

Timon searched Luke's face for any sign of guile. He found none. Could this man really care what happened to him? Timon considered the constant care and concern Luke had shown him in the past week. Could he be trusted?

Ignoring Luke's question, Timon asked, "What's this Christianity about anyway? You're not a Jew. Why do you follow a dead Jewish prophet?"

"Jesus is not dead. It is true, the Romans crucified him, but he has risen. There are many witnesses to both his resurrection and his ascension into heaven. And he's not just a Jewish prophet. He is the Son of the one and only God. He came to earth to offer hope and eternal life, not just to Jews but to all mankind and that includes you, my young friend."

As Luke explained his faith and the joy he had found in life as a child of God, Timon reluctantly felt a growing trust. Hope grew inside his aching chest in response to the warmth and love this stranger seemed to offer.

"Do Christians really help those who are in trouble?" Timon asked.

"We try. We willingly share what we have, but more important, we try to help you solve your own problems by learning to look at life and the world with different eyes...Jesus' eyes. Solutions are often easier to find when seen from His point of view."

"Will you help me even though I'm not a Christian?"

"Yes, if I can, and if what you ask of me is not against God's will."

"Good. Bring me a knife."

"A knife? Why do you want a knife?"

Timon grinned. I'm going to put your Christianity to the test. I'll trust you with some information that could cost me my life. In turn, you must trust me to keep my word not to use the knife to harm anyone and to return it to you next time you come."

"Luke searched Timon's face for a moment. "Why... and what information?"

"First, the information. You're right. I do have the pearls now, but you must believe me, I did not steal them." Step by step, Timon recounted the story. "So you see, if Cassius finds the pearls on me, he will kill me and return them to Marcellos to claim the reward. I need the knife to hide them. Cassius won't kill me as long as he doesn't know where the pearls are hidden. Now, Christian, what will you do?"

Luke's eyes seemed to probe Timon's very heart. Then he spoke, "You drive a hard bargain. You've trusted me with your secret. I will trust you to keep your word about the knife. But there's one more thing. I have listened to your story. Now, you must promise to listen to what I have to tell you about Jesus my Lord."

Chapter 4

The surgical blade Luke had loaned him and the small ball of pitch from the stores locker brought renewed hope. Timon quietly slipped deeper into the darkness of the hold. When he reached the main mast, anchored deep in the heart of the ship, he carefully carved out a small hallow in the towering timber. He searched the hem of his cape until he found the lumps formed by the concealed pearls.

Carefully he slit the stitching. For a moment he gazed at the soft inner glow as the awesome treasure seemed to come alive in the flickering lamp light. To possess these baubles of beauty, Cassius had been willing to risk everything... his position in the house of Marcellos, even imprisonment or slavery had he been caught. He had lied and beaten a fellow human without cause. Now Cassius was willing to commit murder to hide his crime and regain the pearls.

Marcellos would not easily forgive this theft. Aulus Vitellius had chosen the pearls as a gift. Now Marcellos' integrity would be questioned by the procounsel.

Like an echo from the past, Timon could almost hear his father's voice. "Nothing in this world is as valuable as your personal integrity."

His anger flared and he spoke aloud. "You pay a high price, Cassius. Not only have you given up your own integrity. You've tried to steal mine as well. For that, you'll get nothing in return." Quickly he fitted the pearls into the hollow he had carved in the mast and carefully sealed the hole with pitch.

Overhead in the pilot's cabin, Julius silenced the din of arguments that filled the small space. "Enough of this.

We have a serious decision to make, and each of you has a stake in that decision. Captain Nikkos, as owner of the vessel, has the most to lose. The pilot is here because of his knowledge of navigation in these waters. Cassius claims to be an agent of the House of Marcellos and responsible for the cargo that firm has aboard this ship. I, as representative of Rome, have commandeered the services of this vessel and am responsible for the safe delivery of the imperial prisoners aboard."

"We all understand that, Julius, but what is this Jew doing here? We don't need a criminal listening to this."

"Cassius, do you presume to sit in judgment on Paul instead of Caesar? Or perhaps you would like to inform the emperor that you have already judged this case for him." Julius waited for the sting of his sarcasm to have its full effect. At last he continued.

"Paul and his companion, Luke, have traveled widely in this area and may have information which could be useful. Further, I believe Paul has a special relationship with the god he serves. In view of our desperate situation, some divine assistance may be all that can save us. You all know the storm we have just passed through. I doubt we can hope to reach Italy now. We must find a place to winter and wait for the weather to improve."

Captain Nikkos stood, shaking his head emphatically. "Listen to me, Julius. Fair Havens is too small a harbor. They cannot accommodate both the passengers and the crew. There's no place to lock up the prisoners, and not enough food available for all of us. They don't have the facilities I need to repair the damage the storm has done to the ship."

"What about Lasea?" Julius asked. "Is there anything there?"

"Lasea is five miles inland from the port and just a small town. It has even less to offer than Fair Havens. I say we go on."

Thank you, Captain." Julius turned to the pilot. "What do you say? Can you steer us across the Adriatic to Italy this late in the season?"

"It took us nearly fifteen days to cover the one hundred seventy miles between Myra and Cindus and another five days to get here. It's October and you know what Roman sailors say. ' Mid-September, wind and doubt. Mid-October, hear death shout.'

I agree with Captain Nikkos. Fair Havens is no place to winter. I think we can sail on up the coast to Phoenix. It has the only protected harbor on the south side of Crete. It also has accommodations for ships of our size."

"Thank you, pilot. Paul, you have traveled widely in the empire and you seem to receive guidance from your god. How do you view our chances?"

"The pilot is right in saying the season is late. We are already five days beyond the Jewish Day of Atonement which my people believe is the latest a ship can safely sail these waters. We have already lost much time. It has been dangerous getting this far. If we go on, I see that our voyage will end in disaster. It will bring about great loss to both ship and cargo and perhaps our lives as well. We should not leave Fair Havens but make do with such as the area has to offer. We must wait until the storm season has passed."

"He's a prisoner. He just wants to delay his arrival in Rome. Why should we listen to him?" asked the pilot.

Julius pondered his decision in silence for several moments before speaking. "We all agree that Fair Havens is not an ideal winter harbor. All agree that we cannot hope to reach Italy this late in the season. The pilot believes we can reach Phoenix safely. Only Paul objects to that. My decision is to sail along the coast until we reach the harbor at Phoenix and winter there."

The late autumn dawn broke into a clear sky. A gentle southerly wind filled the twin sails of the Aries as Captain Nikkos set a northerly course along the coast of Crete. Julius accepted their congratulations on a good decision as the tiny harbor of Fair Havens faded into the distance. Only Cassius complained. "I say you're all cowards. With a breeze like this we should head straight for Rhegium. A few days after that, we'd be in Rome. I want it understood that when we get to Phoenix I am leaving this ship and taking my prisoner with me."

"Your prisoner?" Julius asked. "I thought I was the only one with authority to hold prisoners on this vessel."

"You know who I mean...Timon, that stowaway slave. I have a score to settle with him."

"Then you'll settle it under Roman law, my friend. You have shown me no authority from your master to take this slave. I thought your mission was to act as agent for Marcellos' interests in Rome. Besides, Captain Nikkos has prior claim on that runaway. Since he's a stowaway aboard this ship and has received food, lodging and care, he will be put to work as a crew member to earn his passage as soon as the physician says he is well enough. Now, why don't you go below and check on your cargo. I am tired of your complaints."

Frustration and festering anger spread across Cassius' mind like a poison as he stalked away from Julius. At the stern of the ship Paul spoke with the Greek physician. Cassius paused a moment as he watched them. Suddenly the rage on his flushed face faded. His lips curved in a cruel smile as he made his way purposefully below decks and into the hold.

The point of Cassius' knife bit into Timon's throat and he jerked into alarmed wakefulness. "Quiet, slave, or you die right here." Timon froze as he recognized Cassius' menacing voice. "It would be a simple matter to cut your throat and throw you overboard. No one will doubt my story when I tell them I saw you escaping in the life boat. Now, it's time we made a deal. If you will give me the pearls, I'll leave the ship at our next port. I'll even help you slip off the ship when we get to Phoenix. You can make good your escape. Marcellos will never know what happened to you.

Slowly Cassius released the pressure of the knife on Timon's throat. "But I didn't steal the pearls, Cassius."

"Of course you didn't, fool. I did. But you stole them from me and now I want what's mine." He emphasized each word with the point of the knife.

"Cassius, I didn't take anything from you. What makes you think I have them?"

"Simple. You and that old fool, Alexos were the only ones at Marcellos' villa the night I took them. You must have seen me hide the pouch under that paving stone. Alexos is still there, but you ran away. When the pearls were gone, I knew it had to be you."

Timon choked off his denial. If Cassius thought Alexos had the pearls, he wouldn't hesitate to kill the old man to find their location. "You're only half right Cassius. I took the pearls with me but I don't have them now."

Cassius struck him full across the face. "Don't play games with me. It's over. Give me the pearls or you die here and now."

"That wouldn't be very smart." The calmness of his own voice surprised Timon. He pushed the knife away from his throat. "If you kill me, you will never have the pearls. I'm the only one who knows where they're hidden. I'm the only hope you have of ever getting them back. You see, I know you Cassius. Your hatred of me is strong, but not as strong as your greed."

Pain exploded like flashes of lightening in the darkness of the hold as Cassius struck Timon again and again, aiming always at his injured rib cage. Methodically then, Cassius began his search. First he stripped Timon of his garments. Then he roughly probed the bandages with which Luke had wrapped the injuries. As Cassius rolled him from the pallet which had been his bed, Timon's hand closed around the cold metal of the blade Luke had loaned him.

"So, you did have the pearls." Cassius snarled. "I can see where they were sewn into the hem of your cape. What have you done with them? Tell me now or you will feel my blade as well as my fists."

"No. Please don't. They're right over there. Timon tightened his grip on the slender knife concealing it in his palm as he pointed to a dark corner. "I hid them in a crack in the floor plank." As Cassius stooped to peer into the darkness, Timon's eyes focused on the curved spinal column.

"Can I help you find something? Let me bring a lamp." Luke's calm voice shattered the tension.

Cassius stumbled to his feet. "What are you doing down here, Greek?"

"I'm here to check on my patient. What 's your interest in him?"

'"That's none of your concern. I'm a free man and don't have to answer to any slave physician."

"Quite true, Cassius. And since you are a free man, I presume you'd like to remain one. I suggest you seriously consider the consequences of any action against the property of Rome. Since this ship sails under the authority of Julius, a centurion who out ranks even the captain, all aboard are now under Roman law. That includes you, me and even this runaway slave."

Cassius stormed from the hold shouting over his shoulder, "Be careful, physician. Accidents happen aboard ships, even to the property of Rome."

Luke spent the night in the hold tending his young patient. After he had tightened the bandages on Timon's chest, he asked. "Do you feel well enough to walk on the upper deck? There's a calm sea this morning, and you need to strengthen your leg muscles. By the way, do you have something to return to me?"

Timon grinned as he retrieved the knife and handed it to Luke. "I've kept my word, Christian."

"Yes, I see. What kept you from using it on Cassius?"

"I almost did. But I had made a promise to you. Somehow I just couldn't. I'd have been no different than he is if I'd killed him with it."

"That's two steps in the right direction. You've honored your word to me and refused to let someone else choose how you behave. Someday you may even learn to treat your enemy as you would want to be treated."

"That's a strange idea. Where did you learn that?"

"Come on. There's someone I'd like you to meet."

"Lead the way. I'm beginning to feel like a trapped rat down here." Timon stood up carefully testing his legs.

"Easy now." Luke steadied Timon as a wave of dizziness swept over him. You haven't been on your feet for several days. Lean on my shoulder."

By the time they had reached the upper deck, Luke detected a slight change in the wind's direction. The calm sea of the morning was now dappled with white caps. Waves began to build before a wind that quartered to the north.

Timon shielded his eyes against the glare of the sun. "Where are we and where are we going?"

"We've left the harbor at Fair Havens and are sailing up the coast of Crete toward the harbor at Phoenix. Julius has decided we will winter there and wait for the stormy season to pass before we sail to Rome.

"How did Cassius like that decision?"

"From what I hear, he didn't like it, but he's only a shipping agent so his opinion doesn't count for much."

"That's not why he's on board. He's after me. He'll try to get the pearls from me. If he can't, I'm sure he will try to kill me. He can't take the chance I might return to Marcellos with the truth. I'm afraid he'll try to take me off the ship when we get to Phoenix."

"I wouldn't worry much about that. My friend Paul says we'll never reach Phoenix. He tried to convince Julius to stay in Fair Havens, but he was out voted."

"Out voted?" I thought he was a prisoner. How can he have anything to say about the way the ship is run?"

"Paul is a great deal more than a prisoner. He's a Roman citizen and an apostle of our Lord Jesus Christ. Julius has great respect for him."

"But how could he know this ship will not make it to Phoenix? Besides, if we don't make that harbor, where will we go?"

"Don't you understand? Paul has committed his life to the will of our Lord. He prays to God for guidance. His prayers are answered. I believe our Lord guided Paul to warn Julius and Captain Nikkos. I don't know where we will go, but you should know this: Paul says this ship will never make any harbor. It will be wrecked."

"Wrecked? If your God can show Paul the future…I mean if this really happens, I guess I'd about have to believe in Him. But if we're shipwrecked, what happens to us? Are you telling me we're all going to drown?"

"I don't believe we are going to drown, but if Paul says we will be shipwrecked, I know it will happen. I also know that the Lord has told Paul he will testify of his faith before even kings. That's why Paul is being sent to testify before Caesar himself. God will not allow anything to prevent that. Not even a shipwreck."

"How can you be so sure?"

"It's called 'faith,' Timon. I know my Lord. I know the power of His might, the force of His will and His love for His children. He loves you too, you know."

"Well, there are plenty who don't love me. You can start the list with Cassius. I've got to get away from him. I have to find some way to escape."

"Don't do anything foolish. Think about the things I have told you. God does love you. If you can learn to trust Him, He will help you find a way to solve your problems. Running away won't help. Problems have a way of following you. You'd better go below now. Its getting cold up here and the wind is kicking up the waves.

A crewman was injured yesterday, and I need to tend to him. Can you make it on your own?"

"Sure. I'm fine, but I'd like to hear more about Paul and this God who foretells the future."

"I'll see that you do hear more. That's a promise. When you're feeling up to it, I'll take you to meet my friend. He's met the Lord in a vision. I think his story might interest you."

Chapter 5

Timon pondered Luke's words as he watched the ship's lifeboat being jerked along by its tow rope behind the ship. Shipwrecked? And that wretched little boat is all that stands between rescue and drowning for nearly three hundred people aboard this ship? Luke is out of his mind if he thinks that's going to happen. As Timon reviewed the day's events, he shuddered at the threats Cassius had made. Then something Cassius had said flitted through his mind. "No one will doubt my story if I tell them I saw you escaping in the lifeboat."

"Well, Cassius, you have been more helpful than you know," he said aloud. As his eyes measured the distance between the tethered boat and the ship, Timon began planning his escape.

"Hey Timon, on deck there. Captain Nikkos wants to see you." The voice of Heru, Captain Nikkos' steward broke into Timon's thoughts. "You better get up there quick. The Captain doesn't like to be kept waiting. A storm's moving in and he needs a crewman to replace the guy who broke his hand."

Timon followed Heru across the heaving deck to the pilot house where the captain was shouting orders to reef the mainsail. When he turned around, he examined Timon with practiced eyes. "So you're our stowaway? I saw you on deck with the physician. If you're well enough to be on deck, you're well enough to earn your keep. There's no free ride on this vessel. Know anything about ships?"

"A little, sir. I often helped to load them for Marcellos and I used to sail with my father."

"You look strong enough to make a deck hand. I'm short a crewman, and you can earn your passage by taking his place. If this storm is what I think it is, you will indeed earn it, if you survive. Watch your step out there. If you are swept overboard, you're fish food. No lifeboat will be wasted on the likes of you. If you make me a good hand, I'll keep you on until we reach Rome. If not, I'll turn you over to Cassius when we reach Phoenix and be glad to be rid of you both."

Gesturing to his steward he said, "Show him to his station, Heru."

As Timon turned, to follow Heru, he heard the pilot's shout above the roar of the sea. "Wind's moved a quarter to the east, Captain. She's east-northeast and rising."

On deck crewmen had strung lifelines about the ship to keep from being thrown or washed overboard. Clinging to the lines with one hand, they worked with the other as they struggled to batten down the ship for the coming storm. Behind the ship the lone lifeboat leaped and tossed as the seas battered it.

Under the watchful eye of his seaman-tutor, Timon performed his assigned tasks with reasonable skill and honest effort. "You're doing all right for a landsman," Heru encouraged, "but watch your step. Things are going to get worse before they get better. If the captain doesn't change course soon, he'll kill us all."

"Change course? I thought we were going to Phoenix."

"We were headed that way, but now we're sailing into the teeth of a gale. Ever hear of the Euroquilo.?"

"No. What's that?"

"You're about to find out. It's a demon wind that can blow for days at hurricane force. It drives the sea in front of it like a wall of water. There's not a ship afloat that can survive if it gets caught in it."

"Doesn't the captain know that?"

"Oh, he knows all right. He's holding the ship on this course long enough for us to secure the deck and cargo. Then he'll run before the storm. I say he was a fool to leave Fair Havens."

Timon smiled as he listened to the young Egyptian. The tone of his voice had changed from pompous officiousness to companionable conversation even as he shouted over the roar of the wind. Heru was obviously enjoying an opportunity to demonstrate his superior knowledge to someone his own age. "I think he was tricked by the good weather we had at Fair Havens, and he sailed without preparing for the worst. Now, here we are on deck, paying the price for his carelessness."

As the storm increased its fury, wind howling through the rigging made further conversation difficult. Finally, Heru signaled that their task was finished. As he turned and pointed toward the hold, the ship shuddered and rolled. Tons of water crashed onto the slanting deck, tearing away a deck stanchion which secured the lifeline Heru was holding. Timon watched in horror as watery claws grasped his new friend tossing him into the air like refuse. As the wave receded, he caught a glimpse of Heru's body sweeping toward the lower edge of the slanting deck, his lifeline trailing behind him.

"Hang on," Timon shouted. Catching the slack line he quickly wrapped it around his shoulders as Heru reached the edge of the deck. The secured rope went taut with the weight of Heru's body and vibrated like a lute string. Timon groaned as his body absorbed the impact. Water clawed at his footing trying to drag him from his feet. The ship struggled for buoyancy as tons of water fell back into the yawning trough of the wave. Ignoring the agony in his chest, Timon began reeling in the line, dragging Heru, like a netted fish, across the deck toward the stanchion that secured their lives.

Clinging to Timon's neck, Heru gasped out his gratitude and relief. "I owe you my life, man. You could have been swept overboard too. Why would you risk your life for me?"

"What kind of question is that? You needed help, and I gave it to you. Anyone would have done the same."

"You're wrong about that. No one on this ship would risk his life for me. I won't forget this."

They struggled against the gale and the rolling deck as they made their way toward the hold. The timbers of the great ship groaned as it turned its stern to the storm. "Let's go below," Timon shouted. "The Captain must have ordered her to run before the wind. There's nothing more we can do here. Besides, you look pretty battered. I think the physician should have a look at you."

Below decks rumors fueled the fears of exhausted men. Around them timbers creaked and moaned as the ship absorbed the relentless assault of the wind and sea driving Aries before it. "I know these waters," whined an old man. "We'll be driven aground on the sand bars of Syrtis. The ship will wreck, and we'll all be drowned. The Captain is beguiled by sea demons. He's carrying us all to our death."

"And you are a fool, old man." The voice of the bo'sun cut through the gloom. "Perhaps the Captain should have listened to the Jewish prophet, but he did not. Now he does the best he can. He runs before the wind. We are now on the lee of the island of Cauda.

Listen…can't you hear? The waves do not beat down on us with such force as before. The island serves as a windbreak. Now we can prepare the ship to fight the storm. On deck, the lot of you. First Watch, bring in the lifeboat from the stern before the wind crushes our hull with it. The rest of you come with me. We need keel lines, and tackle if this ship is to survive. Move. Your lives depend on it."

"What are keel lines?" Timon asked as they made their way to the deck.

"Look at the joints of the ship where the timbers come together." Heru said, "See? They're beginning to separate. In weather like this the ship is bent and twisted. Joints can pull apart. Once they loosen, a rough sea can tear even a ship of this size into nothing but pieces of wood. Keel ropes run under the ship and around its frame. We fasten and tighten them on deck. It helps hold the ship together and gives it strength. It's tough and dangerous work, but it's necessary. You'll see."

On deck the wind was still a gale, but the small island of Cauda rising between the ship and open sea gave them some protection. At the stern, Timon could see the lifeboat being hoisted aboard and inverted on the deck where it could be lashed down. Well, he said to himself, there goes my last hope of escape. He had little time for despair. Under the careful eye of the bo'sun, the brutal work of passing huge water soaked lines under the ship began.

Two teams of men, each handling the heavy lines, threw a loop over the stern and carefully worked the line outward toward the midsection of the ship. Waves swirled around them often forcing the ropes backward losing precious distance. They worked gradually from the midsection toward the stern securing and tightening arm-sized lines around the ship. Then they reversed the process working forward toward the prow.

The rising wind and growing waves repeatedly knocked crewmen to the deck as they struggled to tie off the last of the lines near the prow of the besieged vessel.

As the last line was tightened and secured, weary sailors cheered and turned to find what rest they could below decks. They were stopped by the bo'sun frantically waving his arms and pointing to the sea anchors and gesturing toward the water below. Obediently, the exhausted crew threw the anchors overboard. Timon felt the jolt as the cables took hold, but there seemed to be little change in the pitch and roll of the ship.

"What's that all about?" Timon asked Heru when they reached the crew's quarters.

"Not a good sign," Heru replied. "When the captain orders sea anchors out in weather like this, he's given up holding the ship on any kind of course. All he can hope to do is keep the ship from being driven onto a reef or some island. The sea anchors will slow the ship and keep it running before the storm. Little good that will do, I'm afraid. Already the visibility is so bad you can see nothing but waves." Timon could hear the edge of fear in his friend's voice.

Each passing hour brought higher seas. Despair began to grip the crew as hunger and exhaustion took their toll. Still the winds raged, and island sized waves continued to batter the ship.

As the second day slipped into the third the bo'sun once again called for the crew. "We're taking on water. We have to lighten the ship. Captain Nikkos has ordered the cargo to be thrown overboard. We'll save only enough grain to feed us. Julius has ordered his prisoners to help. I want all cargo holds emptied of every bag, basket and crate."

The crew stood paralyzed by the bo'sun's orders. Fear gripped them. Each man knew the great cost of such an order. A shipload of grain was an enormous fortune in Italy. Only the gravest of circumstances would make a ship owner order it thrown over the side.

"Move it. Do you want to drown like rats in this hold. Get to it," the bo'sun shouted.

Timon was unsure the men would have moved at all if Julius, with his armed guard and prisoners had not arrived to help. Like men in a trance, the weary crewmen began dumping the cargo, lifting heavy bags, crates and amphora, moving them from shoulder to shoulder and finally into the mouth of the hungry sea.

With the cargo gone, the tired ship rode higher on the waves, but with the ballast of the cargo missing, its pitch and yaw grew steadily worse.

"Where do you think we are now?" Timon asked Heru.

"Not even the captain knows that. There's been neither sun nor stars to guide us since this storm began. We're lost at sea. The gods are angry with us. This ship will go down, taking us to the bottom with it."

"Things look bad, I know, but I'm not willing to give up. I was talking to that physician, Luke, and he says his God will protect Paul, His prophet."

"And you believe that? Paul's no prophet. He's just a Roman prisoner."

"I don't know what to believe, but I know those men are different from other men. Even Julius treats them with respect."

"Well, I wouldn't count on it. I was in the pilot house when Paul was talking to the captain. He told him we would lose all the cargo and even the ship. That doesn't give me much hope."

"It all depends on the way you look at it. Paul said that while the weather was clear and we had no problems. Now look at us. It's all happening just as Paul said it would."

"Well, I guess you have to believe in something. Right now, the only thing I would believe in is a hot meal. I'm starving. The dried food is all gone or ruined. All we have left are a few bags of grain. That doesn't sound like this god cares about what happens to us."

Timon and Heru drifted into a troubled sleep dreaming of warm sunny days and steaming food. But their relief was brief.

"Deck crew. Meet me in the forward hold. Hurry up." The bo'sun kicked the bare soles of the sailors feet to make sure they were awake. "Move out now. I need you in a hurry."

"What now? What does he want with a deck crew?" Heru complained.

"The way to find out is to go see, I guess." Timon moaned as he pulled himself to his feet.

In the hold, the bo'sun's voice was grim as he spoke. "The ship is still taking on water, and the storm shows no sign of letting up. We have to lighten the ship as much as possible. I want you to throw overboard every piece of tackle that is not being used. That includes extra sails, spars, rope, and anything that is not necessary to keep the ship afloat. If it isn't attached or being used, throw it overboard."

With each piece of tackle and equipment went the tattered hopes of the sailors. The last shred of confidence was stripped from them. Some resigned themselves to a watery grave and lay down to await their fate. Others raged with anger and threatened mutiny. Timon folded his arms about his knees and rested his head, thinking about his life and the circumstances that had brought him here. "And I told Alexos I'd rather be dead than be a slave. I guess I'll get a chance to see if that's true."

Bonded by crisis, Timon and Heru shared their life stories. "And to think I'm here because of some miserable pearls. If Cassius hadn't stolen the pearls… If I hadn't been beaten and run away…"

A gentle hand on his shoulder interrupted him. "Timon, its Luke. How are you feeling?"

"Luke? What are you doing down here?"

"I came to check on my patient. Is your chest still bound tightly?"

"What difference does that make? We're all going to die anyway."

"Have a little faith, my friend. I told you God wouldn't abandon us. I still believe that."

"Well, he'd better do something quickly. If he doesn't, this crew is going to cut Captain Nikkos' throat and take over the ship. And even if they don't, they will just lie down and die. Look at them. They've given up hope. What's the use?"

"Could you get these men to move into the large center hold? I'd like for Paul to talk to them. I think he can make them feel better about their situation."

"I suppose I could try. Maybe they will listen to Heru if they won't listen to me."

"Good. I want all of the other people on the ship to be there too. I'll see you in the center hold as soon as you can get the men in there."

Timon and Heru moved through the crew's quarters encouraging the sailors to at least listen to what Paul would have to say. Some went out of curiosity to see the famous prisoner. Others, grasping any hope, no mater how fragile, went seeking some inner strength with which to face the coming doom.

A few flickering candles lit the gloom of the empty hold. When all had gathered, Julius, spoke. "Captain Nikkos, crewmen, soldiers and prisoners, you know our situation is desperate, and we have little hope. Paul, my prisoner has asked to speak to you to give you encouragement. Listen to what he says. I believe he speaks with foreknowledge given him by his God."

As Paul stood, an expectant hush fell over the weary men. In his face they found a bright confidence and determination. As the flame of a lamp draws a moth, so this man's presence drew others to him easing their weariness and despair and giving them hope.

"To those in charge of the ship I say, you should have listened to my advice when I told you not to sail from Crete. If you had, you would have spared yourselves this great damage to the ship and the loss of its cargo. But that is done. Now I urge you to keep up your courage. Not one of you is going to lose your life. This ship will be destroyed but you will all live. This was revealed to me last night by an angel of the God to whom I belong and whom I serve. The angel stood beside me and told me not to be afraid. He said, 'You are to stand trial before Caesar. God, in his graciousness has given you the lives of all who are sailing with you.' So be encouraged men. Because of my faith in God, I know this will happen exactly as I've been told. Even though this is true, this ship will run aground and be destroyed, but all of us will survive."

A sense of peace settled over the frightened crew as they listened to Paul's words. Slowly hope-filled voices began to question friends. Here and there excited voices congratulated one another on the coming rescue. Perhaps there would be a tomorrow after all.

Chapter 6

The full force of the storm struck the ship shortly before the midnight watch. Timon, asleep on his cape, was flipped across the hold like a particle of dust from a rug. Throughout the ship exhausted men protested their rude awakening with moans and curses. Screams and fear-filled shouts echoed through the hatch as the unwary were thrown into bulkheads and the rib structure of the besieged ship. Bones snapped like brittle pottery as fear again gripped the crew. Overhead the weary steersman fought to hold the ship into the teeth of the wind.

"It's hopeless, Captain. The men are exhausted. We are at the mercy of the sea." The bo'sun's voice echoed his despair.

"Then tie off the rudder and order the prisoners and soldiers to work the ship." Captain Nikkos commanded. "Our only hope is to keep our heading into the waves. If we are hit broadside by one of these giants, the ship will be swamped or snapped in two like a piece of dry straw. I'll not give up my ship without a fight in spite of what that Jewish prophet says."

Side by side, through the weary hours of the night, sailor, soldier, and prisoner alike worked the ship. The sea had become a personal enemy, a living monster intent on swallowing the feeble beings that floated on its waves.

"Heru, we just seem to be going one direction and then the other. First the wind is from the bow, and then it's from the stern. What's happening?" Timon shouted to his friend.

"It's the way the storm blows. The captain just steers into the next wave. Do you still believe what Paul said? Do you think we can survive this?"

"I don't know. But if it turns out as he said it would, I'll sure believe in his God. Only an all-powerful god can save us now. What about you?"

Before Heru could answer the bo'sun's shout reached them. "Hey, you two. I need a sounding. There's the smell of land in the air. Hurry up. I don't want to be driven onto some pile of rocks only to drown in the sight of land."

As they raced toward the bow of the ship, Heru paused at a rope locker and pulled out the weighted sounding line. "I'll throw it out. You follow it to midship and read the knots," Heru instructed. "Shout out the reading so the bo'sun can hear you."

Timon watched as Heru skillfully whirled the weight overhead and hurled it in an arch into the sea. Coil by coil, the rope was swallowed by the dark depths. Then it stopped. Timon read the depth knot and shouted. "Fifteen feet." As he translated the Roman measure into the more familiar Greek cubit, he was surprised by the shallowness of the reading.

Heru repeated the sounding. "Count twenty breaths and give me the reading again. If it shallows, pull the line and get to the stern. We'll have to put out the last four sea anchors to keep us from running aground."

Heru coiled the sounding rope as Timon counted each breath on his fingers. "Now." He yelled. Once again Heru swung the weighted rope overboard. Crewmen nearby stopped their work and listened for Timon's reading. "Ten feet," Heru shouted.

"Stern anchors out," ordered the bo'sun. "Be quick about it."

Caught up in the urgency of the order, Heru raced toward the stern of the ship. Ahead he noticed Paul talking to the Centurion. As the men frantically heaved the anchors overboard, Timon counted each anchor to himself. As each took hold, the ship slowed perceptibly. As the fourth anchor went overboard a sense of hopelessness settled over the crew as they made their way toward mid-ship. There, Timon noticed a small cluster of men furtively watching as they talked together.

"What are they up to?" he asked Heru.

"I guess they're putting out the last anchor."

"No, the bo'sun said there were only four left and we've already dropped four."

You're right. Look. They're pretending to pull out another anchor, but they are cutting loose the lifeboat. I think they're planning to abandon ship. Quick. I'll try to stop them. You go tell the centurion."

Timon paused a moment recalling where he'd last seen Julius. Spotting the tall Roman still talking with Paul, he ran toward them. "Julius. Some of the sailors are trying to launch the lifeboat and abandon ship.

"Well let them. That boat is of little use to us anyway."

"No." Paul's firm voice rang with authority. "Stop them," he shouted to Julius as he began running along the deck toward the cluster of sailors. "Unless you men stay aboard this ship, you will all be drowned."

Timon watched as the fear-driven sailors turned toward Paul. "Keep out of this, prophet. You have no authority over us. Don't you know what Romans do to prisoners on a sinking ship? If you had any sense, you'd be helping us."

The measured beat of a running cohort and Julius's order, "Swords, ready," froze the sailors as they balanced the boat at the edge of the deck. "Cut the ropes, and let the boat fall into the sea." In response, the squad of soldiers slashed the restraining ropes as the dispirited sailors watched the lifeboat disappear into the yawning maw of an oncoming wave.

Turning to the group that had gathered and including the dejected sailors in his beckoning gesture, Paul spoke. "Look men. There dawns the fourteenth day of our journey. During much of this time, you've been watching and waiting and have had nothing to eat. Please, I beg you. Eat something. You must have food if you are going to stay alive. You must believe me. Not one of you will loose so much as a hair from your heads in this ordeal."

Timon watched in amazement as the force of Paul's words penetrated the hostility and fear surrounding the group. Then, calmly, Paul pulled a piece of dried bread from his robes and held it before the men. In a clear voice he offered thanks to God for the food. Then he broke a piece from the loaf and began to eat. Fear melted as one by one, the men began eating from their meager stores. Soon all two hundred seventy-six people aboard the ship had eaten.

In the grey dawn, Julius called out. "Our stern anchors are holding. Dump the remaining grain into the sea to lighten the ship as much as possible. If you look to the west, you can make out a landfall. That line of white means there are waves hitting a beach. We are going to try to reach it."

Here and there, cheers and shouts greeted his announcement. For others who did not swim, the distant line between sky and water offered scant hope for survival. But it was something where there had been nothing before. The discipline of life at sea asserted itself as the sailors responded to the bo'sun's orders. "On the stern there...cut the anchor ropes. Release the rudder." As the ropes were cut, the great ship, free from its restraints leapt forward toward the line of white water edging the distant beach.

In the pilot house Captain Nikkos shouted. "I need steerage. Order the foresail to be raised. There seems to be some kind of bay there with an inlet. Steer for that." As the foresheets caught the wind, the great ship gained momentum.

Timon and Heru watched as the features of the unknown land rushed toward them growing more distinct by the moment. "I wonder what this place is." Heru said.

"Who knows? Anyway, it has to be better than this ship has been."

"What will you do, Timon? Try to escape from Cassius?"

"I don't know. I had hoped Captain Nikkos would let me stay with the ship until we reached Rome. Then I could have escaped from there, but now I'll have to make new plans. One thing is certain, I will never go anywhere with Cassius. I was a fool not to kill him when I had the chance."

Timon pondered his plight. If Paul was right, and the ship was going to wreck, should he take the pearls with him? If the pearls were lost with the ship and Cassius knew, Timon realized his life would be in jeopardy.

"What's that?   There below the wave.   Look out. We're going to…"

Heru's warning was never heard.   With a grinding roar, the great ship, driven by waves and wind crashed into the sandbar guarding the entrance to the bay.

Chapter 7

Like a monster's hand reaching up from the sea, the sand bar grasped the lunging ship and held it fast. On deck, prisoners, soldiers and sailors were pitched into a tangled heap among ropes and rigging.

The ship's lurching momentum, now blocked by the sand bar, swept forward into the bow. Then a wave of backlash rolled toward the stern. Timon was thrown to the deck by the first impact. He struggled to gain control of his rolling, sliding body. He pushed aside a tangle of ropes and the body of a sailor who had been knocked unconscious by the crash.

As Timon rolled onto his back, he watched in disbelief as the great central mast, an enormous cedar from the forests of Lebanon, bent like the tip of a whip. It arched across the sky, and with a roar like thunder, it splintered a few feet above the deck. Deep wounds opened showing the red and yellow heartwood of the great timber. Twisted from its roots in the keel, the groaning mast slowly collapsed onto the deck destroying a large section of the bulwark. For a moment the fallen mast teetered, then twisted free and slid into the yawing waves that were swallowing the stern of the ship.

"Legionnaires, queue up." The voice of command cut through confusion on the deck. "Surround the prisoners. Draw swords. The ship is lost. Kill the prisoners to prevent escape." Honed blades grated against sheaths as swords were drawn to execute the bloody command of the squad leader.

Timon shuddered as fear clutched at his throat. He knew military code. Any soldier who allowed his prisoner to escape would pay with his own life. As he watched the soldiers begin their advance on the helpless prisoners, Timon wondered once again about his own status. Was he a prisoner or a member of the crew? Surely they would not kill Paul after all he had done to keep the crew from mutiny during the storm.

"Hold. Any man who touches a prisoner will answer to my sword." The cold command of Julius froze the movement of the entire squad. "These prisoners are not trying to escape."

"But Centurion," the edge of pleading complaint could be heard in the squad commander's voice. "if these prisoners go into the sea they'll all escape. We'll answer to the authorities in Rome. Once they go over the side, there's no way we can control them. We have to kill them for our own protection."

"Don't be a fool, Claudius. Escape? Where are they going to go? That island is their only hope and yours. Already the stern of this ship is being beaten to pieces by the waves. If we are to survive this with our lives, we'll have to keep our wits about us and work together. Paul foretold this shipwreck. He said all of us would live through it. Everything he has said has come to pass. Quickly now. Those of you who can swim, into the sea and make for the beach. The rest of you, look around you. There are pieces of decking and ship timbers in the sea. As you go overboard grab a piece of the wreckage. The surf will carry you to the shore. Now move. We've very little time before this ship is torn to pieces."

As if in response to a command, the ship shuddered and groaned as its keel was broken by the beating waves hammering it onto the sand bar. Soon swimmers bobbed among floating debris as they made their way toward the island.

Timon ran to the tilting edge of the deck. Then he caught sight of Heru hanging onto a piece of planking and staring in horror at the boiling cauldron below them. "Come on. Lets go." Timon shouted.

`"I… I… I can't swim. I'll drown. I can't make it."

"What do you think will happen if you stay here? Can't you see this wreck is going down? Hurry. I'll help you." When Heru made no move, Timon locked his arms around his friend and the plank he clutched. Using their combined weight, he overbalanced them and they tumbled headlong into the sea.

The impact tore Heru from Timon's grasp as the grey water engulfed them. Frantically, Timon struggled against the downward thrust of his body and fought his way back to the surface. Ahead he could see Heru, still grasping the deck plank, floating on the waves. A few swift strokes brought Timon along side his panic stricken friend. "We're fine. We're going to make it. Take it easy. Just hang onto the plank. I'll swim on this side and you kick your feet as I pull you along." Heru nodded his head to signal his understanding. They began to move away from the towering hulk.

Overhead, Julius was shoving the last reluctant prisoners and soldiers over the edge of the tilting deck and into the sea. Timon caught sight of Cassius gesturing wildly. The centurion pointed emphatically toward the sea as Cassius began to back away from him. Clearly exasperated, Julius grabbed the frightened Cassius and hurled him overboard.

An almost human groan rose from the vessel as the keel separated where the main mast had been attached. The planks along the sides began to pull apart as the stern separated from the rest of the ship leaving the stub of the mast still attached to the bow.

The wreckage of the stern section, now free of the grounded ship slipped into the sea. Timon could feel the undertow, like the suction of a giant squid, pulling them backward as water swirled to fill the space left by the floating hulk. "Kick harder. Paddle with your arm. If we get sucked under that wreckage, we'll be killed."

Frantically they struggled against the swirling cross currents dragging them toward the sinking wreck. For a moment the plank seemed to stand still in the sea. Then slowly it began to move again, drawn by the water swirling into the cavern that had been the hold of the Aries. "It's a whirlpool. It's sucking us under." Heru's voice was ragged with terror. "We're going to die."

Timon reached across the plank and grabbed Heru by his hair and shook him. "Listen to me. We are not going to die. The Lord told Paul none of us would be lost, and I believe that. Now use your breath to paddle."

Surprised and startled by Timon's assault, Heru slowly dispelled the terror that gripped him and found comfort in the authority of Timon's instructions. As they fought against the drag of the waves, the plank maintained its distance from the yawning trough. Yet the swirling water held them in its grasp. With concerted effort they began to break free. "Keep it up. We're going to make it."

Another pair of hands had grasped the plank. Timon looked into the calm face of Luke, the physician. As they rose with the oncoming wave, the swirling current released them. The curling white water tumbled them into its trough. When they broke the surface terror had returned to Heru's eyes. "He can't handle much more of this," Timon shouted over the roar of water.

"See if we can get him up onto the plank. We're across the sand bar now and the waves will carry us to shore." Without waiting for Timon's response, Luke draped Heru's limp arms across the plank. Timon grasped them. He guided Heru's head and shoulders as Luke pushed the exhausted Egyptian onto the makeshift raft.

Beyond the sandbar, the graceful neck and head of the golden goose that decorated the once proud ship dipped into the sea like a wounded bird and slowly sank from sight. Broken boards and bits of floating debris bobbed to the surface among great bubbles of air displaced by the water that now filled the dead ship's hull.

Ahead, on the beach, the three exhausted young men could hear shouts of reunion as friends greeted each other and congratulated themselves on their survival. They pulled themselves onto the beach. Just out of the grasp of the waves they rolled onto their backs to rest in the wet sand.

When he could breathe without gasping from exhaustion, Timon spoke. "Luke, I believe what Paul told us. It's happened. But I don't think I could have gotten us both ashore without your help. I don't know whether to thank you or the god Paul worships for our rescue. What made you come back? You left the ship ahead of us."

"You looked like you could use some help. It was His will that none of us would die in the sea. If I was there to help, it was because God often uses His people to carry out His will. Offer God your thanks just as I do."

Heru leaned back on his elbows and wiped the first drops of cold rain from his face. "Well, I thank whatever gods there are for both of you. I'd never have made it alone."

"But don't you see? We weren't alone. Paul's God was with us. Besides, there are no other gods. I stopped believing in those children's stories years ago. Now I believe in Paul's and Luke's God. Only an all-powerful God could have foreseen this and kept his promise to bring us here safely."

Luke shivered in the cold rain as he spoke. "You're only partly right Timon. Jehovah God is with us, but he is not just the God of Paul and Luke. He is your God too. He protected us from the sea, and you have acknowledged him as God. Perhaps it's time for you to consider serving Him as His man."

"You two can sit here in the rain and talk philosophy if you want to. I'm cold. Let's find some shelter," Heru said, getting to his feet.

They stood and brushed wet sand from their bodies. Timon suddenly pointed toward the beach above them. "Someone lives on this island. They're watching us from behind that clump of bushes up there."

Chapter 8

"Quo vadis?" A toga-clad figure, his right hand extended in the Roman greeting, approached.

"That's Latin. He's asking where we are going," Timon said in surprise.

"You'd better identify yourself. He may have soldiers with him," Luke said.

"We are survivors from the ship Aries out of Alexandria under the command of the Centurion, Julius and Captain Nikkos. We were bound for Rome." Timon shouted across the narrowing distance between them.

"I wonder what place this is," Timon said, as the man drew near.

"I doubt that even Captain Nikkos knows that," Luke answered. "After fourteen days in the storm we've lost all sense of distance and direction. But at least that man comes in peace and knows Roman customs."

Timon studied the approaching figure. The man moved with confidence, authority and purpose in every stride. His bearing suggested military training. The sun-darkened face, edged by a graying beard, wore a reserved but friendly smile.

He extended a walking staff and spoke, "I am Quintus, steward of the Honorable Publius, who is chief official on this island by the authority of Caesar." As he spoke, he touched the medallion hanging around his neck. "In his name, I welcome you to Malta."

Luke introduced himself, Timon and Heru. Then he briefly explained their situation. "There were two hundred seventy-six of us aboard the Aries. The others must be further up the beach."

"Yes, you were swept beyond the curve of the bay. The rest of your shipmates are just beyond that sand dune. We saw your ship break up on the sand bar. Some of the local people are helping gather wood for a fire to help fight off the coldness and rain. Come. I'll show you."

At the top of the dune, they looked down on the wide curving beach, now a scene of confused activity. In the distance, Timon recognized the tall figure of Julius as he gave directions and tried to organize the clusters of weary men huddled together for protection. Here and there debris from the broken ship had been leaned, stacked and piled in a feeble attempt at shelter from the driving rain. Island residents were bringing dry wood to start a fire.

"I will leave you here and report the wreck to Publius. He will authorize food and shelter for you. Quintus, giving a respectful nod, strode away toward the rising beach. Beyond, Timon could see the roof line of several large buildings.

They joined the other survivors in seeking wood that had not yet been soaked by the rain. In a sheltered draw between two sand dunes, Timon stooped to pull fallen branches from a clump of bushes. A powerful rough hand grasped his bare shoulder and pulled him to his feet. "So the gods have saved you for my blade, have they?" Timon shuddered as he recognized the hard sneering voice of his enemy, Cassius.

"I think I'll kill you here and now and throw you into the sea. Then I can return to Myra and tell Marcellos you died in the shipwreck taking the pearls with you. There may even be a reward in it for me."

"Then you'll never get the pearls, and you'll probably be charged with destroying Marcellos' property. There are several people who will verify that I reached shore alive."

"So you still have the pearls, do you?" The glint of greed lighted Cassius' face. "My deal still stands. Give them to me, and you can go your way, and I'll go mine."

"Look at me." Where would I hide anything? All I have in the world is this rag of a tunic tied about my waist. But the pearls are not lost. I don't have them with me, but I know where they are and can get them when I want them. Subconsciously, Timon's glance flitted to the tilting prow of the wrecked hulk resting on the sand bar, its broken mast just visible above the water.

" So, they are hidden on that wreck are they? Do you think you are going to get them without me? Whether you like it or not, you now have a partner in crime, my young Greek. Your fate is in my hands. The gods have spared you from death in the sea, but then, the gods are kinder than I am. If you try to escape this island…"

"Come on, you two. Time for a head count. Julius wants everyone over by the fire. Bring your wood along and get moving." Cassius swore under his breath at the soldier's interruption, but released Timon from his grip.

As the soldier turned, he gave a warning. "Watch carefully where you pick up wood. The natives say there is a breed of viper that lives in these shrubs. A bite from one of them will kill a man in a few breaths according to the people who live here."

Gingerly, Timon shook the bundle before lifting it to his shoulder. "Snakes in the bushes and a snake on the beach, he muttered to himself as he made his way down the dune toward the fire.

The chilled survivors ringed the blaze, jostling each other to get near the welcomed heat as Julius organized them into groups accounting first for each soldier and each prisoner in his troop. Heru, standing on a rock beside Captain Nikkos, called out each sailor's name as the captain made tally marks in the sand. "That's twenty-six. All sailors accounted for," he called to Julius.

"And that brings the total to two hundred seventy-six," Julius announced. "Every person on board the Aries has survived just as Paul foretold. If we had listened to him earlier, none of this would have happened. Though, according to law, he is my prisoner, we owe him our respect and honor."

Paul carried a bundle of brush wood which he dropped on the hungry flames before he spoke. "You owe me no honors, Julius. It has happened through the power of Jesus Christ and the all-powerful God I serve. To Him give the honor, glory, and praise."

As Paul pushed the last of the brush into the fire, an angry fanged head raised from the burning sticks, and with the speed of lightening struck, driving twin fangs into Paul's outstretched hand.

"Look. He is an evil man," shouted a resident who had brought clothing to help the survivors. "He has escaped the gods of the sea. Now he will die by the justice of the gods of the island."

"What have you done? He must be a murderer to be so punished." another shouted. "Stand back. He will soon fall dead. Let him fall into the fire and be burned."

Paul calmly looked at each accuser and smiled kindly. "No, my friend. I am no murderer. I serve Jehovah God and am his messenger to share the good news of Jesus Christ to you. He has protected me. No harm will come of this."

Silence engulfed the group. As Paul spoke to them, they watched his hand for the telltale signs of redness and swelling that would surely make a lie of all he had said. But nothing happened. Timon realized he had been holding his breath. He'd recognized the viper as a deadly breed from whose bites humans did not recover. Moving around the edge of the group, he spoke to Luke.

"You're a physician. Shouldn't you treat him?"

"He has no need of my skills. God has protected him. What no physician's skills could do, our God has done with ease."

A low murmur arose from the islanders whose eyes were fastened on Paul's hand. Their cries became a chant. "He is a god. He is a god" Timon was sure they were about to fall to the ground in homage and worship when the strong voice of Quintus broke their awe.

"I bring you greetings in the name of Publius, our governor. All of you are welcome at his estate where you will be given food, clothing and shelter. The officers and dignitaries of the ship are invited to a banquet given in your honor in the main hall tonight. He asks two favors of you. The father of the governor has fallen ill and is in need of a physician. Also, we are an isolated island and have only limited contact with mainland ships. The governor has two children who need a tutor. Is there anyone in your company who is skilled in healing or who could teach language and mathematics in the governor's home until another passage for you can be arranged?"

"Honorable Quintus, this man is a god, a worker of miracles," shouted one of the islanders, pointing to Paul. "We have seen him heal himself of the viper's bite."

As Quintus turned toward him, Paul spoke. "It is Luke who is the physician. I am but a servant of Jehovah

God. However, if you will allow Luke to come with me, we will attend the governor's father."

"Where is the physician?" Quintus asked, scanning the crowd.

"I am Luke." As he stepped forward, Luke drew Timon through the crowd into the clearing before Quintus. "And this is Timon, a Greek, a native of Ephesus, educated in the best schools of that great city. I am sure he will be pleased to use his skills to serve the governor in recognition of his great kindness to us."

"You can't take Timon with you. He's a runaway slave."

"And who are you?" Quintus asked the whining Cassius.

"I am Cassius, servant to the house of Marcellos of Myra. This slave is my prisoner. I'm returning him to my master for punishment."

"Are you leaving immediately?" asked Quintus, his voice heavy with sarcasm. "Or are you telling me you do not trust the governor to return this prisoner to you safely?"

"No, of course not," stammered the embarrassed Cassius.

"Then, if Luke, Paul and Timon will accompany me, each of you can tell me more about your background and qualifications on the way to the governor's estate. The rest of you will be welcomed by Publius personally at the banquet this evening."

Chapter 9

Inside the estate's whitewashed walls, the garden, elegant even in the cold October rain, reminded Timon of his childhood home in Ephesus. Quintus led them through an open atrium into a small waiting room heated by a brazier on a raised platform. Tapestries and an elaborate mosaic depicting a battle decorated the walls.

"If you will wait here, I will report what you have told me to the Honorable Publius. He will see you shortly." With that, Quintus walked down a hallway into the interior of the great house.

"I can't believe this is happening," Timon said as he looked about at the lavishly decorated room. "Will the governor allow someone like me into a house like this even as a tutor? I'm a runaway slave, just as Cassius said."

Paul's blue eyes seemed to bore into Timon's very mind. "Are you still unwilling to trust in God, Timon? Hasn't he brought you to this point safely? Could it be that He has a purpose for your life that you do not yet understand? Luke told me about your situation. As bad as it is, can you not see the hand of God in your life? Aren't you ready to commit your life to Jesus Christ?"

"I do believe in your God. But how could He be interested in me, a slave, a nobody? Besides, doesn't a servant of God have to be a holy person, someone like you?

"You make three common mistakes, my son. First, I am not holy. It is the cleansing blood of Jesus Christ that washes away my sin. I have been the chief of all sinners. But His forgiveness wipes that away and makes me whole and pure in His sight. Second, you are not 'a nobody'.

You are a creation of God. As such He cares for you and loves you as a son. Finally, belief alone is not enough. As a friend of mine says, 'the devil also believes and trembles'.

Look at me. I have believed in the God of my fathers from my earliest remembrance and have tried to serve Him faithfully. Yet I failed to recognize the promised Messiah when God sent Him to earth. I fought against Him and persecuted without mercy those Christians who followed in 'The Way.' Yes. I had them thrown into prison and tortured. Some even considered me an accomplice to murder. I held the coats of those who killed the Lord's faithful servant, Stephen. For that death, I was directly responsible."

The many questions forming in Timon's mind were interrupted by the sound of Quintus' sandals on the chipped rock path leading from the interior of the house into the courtyard. "Publius will see you now. Follow me."

They passed through a great central hall. Carved stone pillars supported the ceiling and rooms on the second floor surrounding the open atrium. Rain slanted through the open courtyard splashing into the pool. As his eyes became accustomed to the darkness, Timon recognized the mosaic artwork so popular in fashionable Roman homes.

Quintus led them through a formal dining area and into a large garden, enclosed on four sides by the private rooms of the family. Even in the winter rain he could smell the scent of carob, sycamore, and pepper trees. Quintus paused before a door of polished cedar, rapped lightly and opened it. Publius, the chief man of the island, sat behind a writing table.

"Honorable Publius, may I present Centurion Julius, and certain of his company from the Aries, an Alexandrian grain ship which wrecked on our coast this morning."

"Welcome. Quintus has told me of your misfortune. It is an all too familiar fate for ships that sail these waters this time of year. Who are these you have brought with you?"

Turning to the three standing behind him, Julius introduced his companions. "Honorable Publius, I present my prisoner, Paul of Tarsus. By his own appeal, he is on his way to Rome to plead his case before Caesar himself. It is through this man and the power of his God that we are here at all. Time and again his wisdom saved us from destruction at sea. Had we listened to him in the beginning, none of this would have happened.

Though he is my prisoner, I respect him as I respect few others in the Empire. In the midst of the storm and throughout our ordeal, he and his friend Luke, encouraged those around them and used their skills to help the sick and injured."

Gesturing toward Timon, he said, "This young man is Timon of Myra. His status is less clear to me. He admits to being a runaway slave. However, he is also accused of being a thief by Cassius, a steward of the house of Marcellos. His behavior is not that of a criminal, and Cassius has no warrant to verify his accusations. I brought him at the request of Quintus since Timon has received a Greek education and is skillful in both mathematics and languages."

"Find seats and I will hear your report, Centurion."

Julius recounted the events of the storm and eventual shipwreck on the island. As he spoke, Timon studied his host, a man who held all their futures in his hand. Publius, dressed in the toga and badges of his office, was a handsome man who reminded Timon of his own father before the disaster in Ephesus. Touches of grey streaked the short black hair. He was clean shaven in the Roman style, and the threat of a smile played at the corners of his mouth. From time to time, he nodded in understanding or interrupted Julius with a question for clarification of some point.

Julius, with typical Roman efficiency, quickly and succinctly described their situation and summarized their needs. "And so, Honorable Publius, our greatest need is for temporary food and shelter and a ship to take us on to Italy. As an officer in the Roman Army, I am authorized to insure payment for any expenses incurred because of our presence here or required for transportation to our destination."

"There is no problem meeting your need for food and shelter. You and your prisoners are welcome here at my estate. There is more than ample space for shelter on this or neighboring estates for those sailors and other passengers. As to transportation, that is not so easy. It is now winter, and even if we had a ship in the harbor, you would find no captain willing to risk a ship in these waters during this season of the year. It will be at least three months before a ship of the size you require will call at our port. After that, there will be no shortage of grain transports sailing for Rhegium or Puteoli. From there, it is only a short journey overland to Rome. In the meantime, accept our island's hospitality. Enjoy what comforts we have to offer. You are invited to a banquet to celebrate your rescue from the sea."

" But now, a personal matter." Pubilus turned as if to appraise Luke. "When Quintus reported a physician among you, I asked that you be brought here with Julius. Quintus reports that Paul was miraculously cured from the bite of a serpent. Perhaps the two of you can help me."

"In what way, Honorable Publius?" Luke asked. "We are at your command."

"Three days ago my father, Flavius, fell ill with a fever and severe dysentery. Each day the fever is higher, and he grows steadily weaker. We have begun to fear for his life. That is why I sent Quintus to find you. Will you attend my father?"

"Of course, Honored Publius. I will do what I can, but from what you describe, there may be little my skills can do. Is your father here?"

"Yes. I will take you to his quarters."

Turning to Quintus, Publius gave further instructions. "I will send Gnaeus and Celia to you, Quintus. Present them to Timon and explain my needs in their regard."

Publius paused at the doorway leading to the family's private rooms. Turning, he spoke his children's names softly and beckoned them into the room. Nodding respectfully to their father, Gnaeus and Celia entered casting curious glances at the strangers in their father's office. The boy, about twelve years of age, was a youthful miniature of his father. He held his head with a pride that bordered on arrogance. Its effect was softened by the twinkle in his dark eyes and the hint of a mischievous grin that played at the corners of his mouth. Sun tanned, well muscled legs extended below the hem of the short toga. Muscles twitched in objection to their confinement indoors.

Timon felt a tightening in his throat as his gaze rested on Celia. Dressed in the formal Roman style, she reminded him of the marble statues decorating the porticos of the temples he had seen when he traveled in Rome with his father years ago. She appeared almost his age, but her dress and hair style suggested she was not yet regarded by her family as having reached maturity. Her hair was dark like her brother's and framed an oval face. Her eyes were the color of polished amber. Her sculptured face had often been touched by the sun and wore a serious and dignified expression. A slightly upturned nose hinted of good humor and hidden mischief.

Quintus's introduction broke Timon's appraisal. "These are the children of the Honorable Publius. It is because of them that the governor asked that I bring Timon to the house as well. Until recently Gnaeus has been the responsibility of his tutor Dionysius, a Greek slave. But after years of faithful service to this house, Publius granted freedom to the old man. He has returned to his original home in Corinth. As I have time, I try to teach this young rascal Roman law and history, but alas, I lack skills in languages and mathematics. He has an alert mind and will soon overtake my knowledge though not my wisdom, judgment, and experience." Quintus smiled fondly at Gnaeus, and ruffled the boy's closely cropped hair.

"This is Celia. Though she is a girl, I must admit she has learned almost as much as her brother, and that by listening at a distance." The Governor is a modern Roman, and for better or worse, has allowed Celia to profit from her brother's instruction. I don't know what good learning will do her when she is married and must manage her own household."

Timon smiled to himself as he listened to the overtones of "old Roman" values cradling the words Quintus had spoken. Then he asked, "Do I understand that the governor is asking me to serve this house as a tutor while we are here?"

"Yes. It has been reported that you are competent in both mathematics and languages. Is this true?"

"I was taught in the finest school in Ephesus and had expected to complete my training at the university in Alexandria." Timon could hear the ring of pride in his own voice. He quickly added. "That was before my household was destroyed and I was sold into slavery. Since that time, I have served Marcellos as an accountant in his shipping firm. I also served as a translator in his negotiations and business with foreign merchants. I am fluent in Greek, Latin, and Egyptian, and have an acquaintance with Hebrew. I am familiar with some dialects of the Province of Asia."

"You made reference to your family. How is it your family was destroyed?"

Timon could feel his face flush with emotion as he carefully framed his answer. "My father served as secretary to Janius Silanus, a proconsul of Asia. That good servant of Rome was poisoned by Romans on his own staff. My father found evidence that implicated a Roman Knight, Publius Celer, and a freedman named Helios. It was my father's misfortune to be an honest and honorable man who assumed others to be honest and honorable as well. He presented his evidence to Roman officials." Timon paused and his jaw muscles twitched as he held Quintus' eyes in a visual grip. "Perhaps I should stop or you may hear information that is not welcome in this house."

Quintus' eyes did not waver. "Continue, young Greek. I am not unacquainted with political intrigue in high places. I am somewhat aware of the situation surrounding the Honorable Proconsul Silanius."

"Very well then. What my father did not know was that those officials were implicated in the plot. He was immediately arrested. Celer and Helios accused him of helping plot the assassination. They executed him in the public forum in Ephesus. Our property was seized, and my mother, my two sisters and I were sold into slavery along with the servants of our household. I was purchased by the House of Marcellos and taken to Myra where I served that house as I have explained."

"Why did you run away. Weren't you treated well by Marcellos? He has a good reputation, even here."

Timon's answer was interrupted. Luke reentered the room followed by Publius who's face was lined with concern and distress. Luke addressed Paul in urgent tones.

"The needs of the old gentlemen are beyond my skills, my brother. I saw many of these cases as I grew up in Antioch. We studied them at the University in Tarsus. When a bloody flux begins, as it has with this old fellow, there is nothing a physician can do. Will you come with us and pray God's help for this man? I have done all I can."

As they approached the bed chamber, Timon recognized the smell of sickness and coming death. Servants stood in the shadows of the room, fearful but still attending the honored elder of the household. Timon shuddered, remembering the plague that had swept the slave quarters at Myra shortly after his arrival. He carefully watched Paul, touched by the wave of compassion that swept over the apostle's craggy features. On the bed a frail and emaciated old man writhed in agony. Kneeling, the apostle began to pray, first expressing praise, adoration and thanksgiving to God for the rescue and hospitality offered by Publius. Then, in the name of Jesus Christ, he asked for healing.

"Use me, oh Father, as a vessel for your grace and power. Restore this one to his family in health that they may know your great compassion. Help them recognize the power of Jesus Christ and His gospel which I preach in His name. Amen."

Paul arose and gently placed his scarred hands on the old man's fevered head and spoke. "In the name of Jesus Christ, arise and be healed."

When Paul stepped back from the bedside, the flushed color of the old man's stubbled face faded. His eyelids fluttered, opened and focused on Paul, still standing over him. "Who are you, and what are you doing in my bedroom?"

"Chaos erupted. Servants fell to their knees shouting, "It's a miracle. He is Paeon, come to heal the master's father." Publius rushed forward, tearfully embracing the old man. Quintus, forgetting his usual formality, grasped Paul's hand and began to congratulate the apostle as the others clustered around in confusion.

"Listen to me." Paul's authoritative voice cut through the noise. "I rejoice with you in the healing of Flavius. But you must stop congratulating me. I am not a god nor is it by my power that this was done. It is in the name of Jesus Christ, my Lord and by His mighty power that this man stands before you, restored and in good health. Let God's name be praised."

Gradually Publius quieted the excited and confused servants. He dismissed servants no longer needed to attend his father. They hurried to share the good news with the rest of the household and to embellish the wondrous tale. Others tended the restored Flavius as he cleaned and dressed himself to rejoin the family. By afternoon word of the healing had spread throughout the island. Those who had seen Paul deal with the serpent at the fire verified the great power they had witnessed.

Back in his office, Publius spoke to Paul. "There is no way I can repay you for what you have done. Were it in my power, I would revoke all charges against you and all your company. You would remain here as my honored guests as long as you would stay. I do not have the authority to do that, but I can assure you that all your needs will be met. You will be well cared for as long as you need to stay. When you are ready to sail on to Rome, we will provide you with all you need to see you safely to your destination. You are a mighty and powerful man though you deny being a god."

"Indeed, I am not a god. There is only one God. Nor am I mighty or powerful. I am but a servant of Jesus Christ." Patiently the apostle shared his faith with Publius. Timon listened to Paul recount his story. Missing pieces of a beautiful picture fell into place. As he listened he understood God's eternal purpose to bring forgiveness, hope, and eternal life to all mankind. In his excitement, he interrupted the apostle with a burning question.

"Then, how did you become a Christian, Paul?"

"On my way to eliminate the Christians in Damascus, Jesus revealed Himself to me and confronted me with my sin. I believed in Him and was obedient to the vision.

With the help of a Christian from Damascus, I was baptized in Christ's name. My sins were washed away, and I arose from the water as Christ arose from the tomb, born again to walk in a new way of life. From that day, I have served my Lord and Savior, Jesus Christ. In His name, I plead with you and Publius, become followers of Christ. Confess your faith in Him. Allow me to baptize you in the pool there in the garden. You can arise from the water, cleansed, new men with a new hope, a new purpose, and a new life in Jesus Christ."

Like a fire, the passionate plea of Paul burned in Timon's heart. Could it be possible? Could God really love even a runaway slave? "Paul, I do believe in Jesus Christ. Will you baptize me?

"I too believe," said Publius. "Will you also baptize a Roman believer?"

After Paul lifted first Publius and then Timon from the water of the garden pool, Quintus spoke from the sheltering atrium. "I have heard of this new faith which is spreading across the empire. You must tell me more about it. Now, however, a great crowd awaits you outside the gates of the estate. They have brought to you their sick from all over the island. They await you, begging for healing."

As they followed Quintus through the long hallways into the great house, Timon was filled with joy and excitement, with a new spirit and a new hope. He did not notice the hate-filled eyes peering at him from behind a latticed screen.

Chapter 10

The rhythm of estate life was as varied as Malta's November weather. Wet, cold and gloomy days were followed by bright sunshine and gentle breezes, air edged with the brittleness of impending change. Timon looked forward to the daily sessions spent in the small garden study set aside for his use by Publius. Dyonesius, the former tutor, had served his master well. Timon found both Gnaeus and Celia well taught in history, logic and rhetoric but somewhat lacking in mathematics. Celia, now past her fifteenth birthday, was not allowed to join her brother for instruction. Timon was well aware of her presence behind the inlaid screen that separated the temporary classroom from the atrium and garden. After lessons were complete she would often join Gnaeus in questioning Timon about life in other parts of the empire and especially about what he had seen in Rome.

"Do the girls of Rome dress as we do?" Celia asked. As she turned, the intricately embroidered stole swirled out from her shoulders. Deliberately, she brushed his face with the full, long sleeves of her winter gown. She let her orange and yellow wrist handkerchief hang tantalizingly before his face for a moment.

"I have had little chance to see the young girls in Rome," Timon stammered, nearly choking on the sudden throbbing he felt in his throat. "And those I saw were slaves in the marketplace. They were nothing like you."

"But were they pretty?" Celia's probing amber eyes caught and held Timon's glance for a moment before he began a serious study of the black and white pattern of the tiles at his feet. A teasing smile played at the corners of her mouth.

"I'm sure none of them were as pretty as you."

" And none of them such a big flirt," teased Gnaeus. "Leave Timon alone. He's going to tell me about some old guy named Hipparchus who studied the stars and the moon. When spring comes, we're going to watch an eclipse of the moon, aren't we Timon?"

"I'm afraid that will depend on whether your father believes Cassius or me. Cassius has already petitioned your father to allow him to take me to Rome or return me to Myra. If I go to Rome I will be punished as a runaway slave. If he takes me back to Myra, I will be punished as a runaway slave and a thief. Either way, I will probably end up branded and chained to an oarlock in a warship or put to death as a troublemaker.

"But you're not guilty. I know you're not. And besides, my father won't let anything happen to you. I heard him tell Quintus that you are a fine tutor. I know he trusts you. If he didn't he wouldn't allow you in our home. You aren't a thief, are you?"

"No, Gnaeus, I am not, but Cassius has made that very hard to prove. He is the thief, but he is a free man, and I am a slave, and I did run away. No one is going to believe me.

"What did Cassius steal?" Celia asked. "And how did he place the blame on you?"

As Timon recounted the events that had led him to his decision to run away, he searched the faces of the two young Romans. In spite of their privileged position as children of the chief official of the island, they recognized injustice. Their indignation was born of the growing friendship they felt for Timon.

"But if you don't have the pearls, how can they say you stole them?"

"That's the problem. I do have the pearls, or at least I know where they are.

Even though I have suffered under the lash for them, they are not mine. I want to return them to my master, Marcellos. But I can't take them back myself. If they are found on me, it will prove my guilt. If Cassius finds them he will kill me and take them back for the reward or he will keep them for himself. I'm a Christian now. I know I should forgive and pray for my enemy. I pray for forgiveness, but I can't help hating that man and wishing him dead.

A household servant coughed softly at the doorway. "What is it, Phoebe?" Celia asked.

"Your mother wants you to attend her in her sitting room, mistress."

"Mother always seems to know when the lessons are over. She never leaves me any time to find out the things I want to know. It isn't fair. Will there be lessons again tomorrow?" she asked.

"Yes. Tomorrow Gnaeus and I will examine a new scroll on mechanics written by Heron of Alexandria. I found it in your father's library."

"Then I won't bother to sit behind the screen. I think that is very dull." With that, Celia whirled around and followed the beckoning Phoebe into the house.

"Timon, today is the first warm day this week. Let's go down to the bay for a swim. Maybe we could swim out to what's left of your ship. The mast and part of the bow are still stuck on the sandbar."

"I'm not sure I want to be reminded of the shipwreck, but a swim sounds tempting. You did well in your lessons today. I guess you deserve a break. After your lunch, get your things together. I will meet you outside the gatehouse when you are ready."

As Timon made his way across the open courtyard, he squinted at the brightness of the sun shining through the open roof onto the garden pool where he had begun his new life as a child of God. He made his way through the shadowed arch of the gatehouse. Outside, he leaned against the white washed wall and waited for Ganaeus.

The day's warmth soaked into his scarred back. Into the hot bright silence, dark and unwelcomed thoughts intruded. The mention of the shipwreck had sharpened the unpleasant memories and the nagging problems he had pushed from his thoughts. He had used his new responsibilities as tutor to cover them, but whenever he was alone or had time to think, they erupted into his consciousness like leprosy. They always left him feeling miserable and unclean.

First, there was the matter of his personal status. He had been treated well by Publius. He was regarded, not as a servant and slave, but as a brother in Christ. That did not change the fact, however, that under Roman law he was still the property of Marcellos. In that household he was still regarded as a runaway slave guilty of theft. Winter would soon be over, and the shipping lanes would open. What then? Cassius was certain to demand the right to return him to Marcellos.

Timon shuddered at the thought, knowing that it was unlikely Cassius would allow him to reach Myra alive. Then there was the matter of the pearls. Even though he had not stolen them, he knew where they were hidden and they could be his for the taking. At one time none of this would have mattered, but now, as a Christian, he knew he must find a solution to the sense of guilt he felt in all this. His thoughts were interrupted by the crunch of sandals on the stone walkway and Timon's thoughts were jerked back to the present.

"Race you to the beach." Gnaeus shouted. Without waiting for his challenge to be accepted, he darted past Timon, his feet kicking up puffs of dust along the sandy path leading down to the sea. Leaping to his feet, Timon raced after his young charge. They arrived at the base of the headland in a tie and rushed into the brown waters of the stream swirling its muddy path into the clear blue basin of the bay.

"Hey, there's not much left of that old ship," Gnaeus said, pointing toward the broken hulk. "And isn't the mast moving back and forth in the waves?"

Timon squinted at the glare of the mid-day sun reflecting on the shimmering blue surface. "You're right. That last storm must have dragged it out of the mud where it was stuck."

"Let's swim out and look at it. If we have another storm, it will be gone. I'd like to get a good look at the old Aries before it's swept out to sea and turned into driftwood. How about it, Timon?"

"That's not a good idea. The floor of the bay drops off quickly beyond the shoal. I remember that from the soundings of the linesman before we ran aground. If we should be out there when the wreck breaks loose, we could be dragged out to sea with it."

"Well, at least, let's swim out that way so I can get a better look at it."

"I guess that would be safe enough, but you have to stay well back on this side of those ripples where the water crosses the sandbar. Let's see how well you can race in the water."

Timon's long, easy strokes soon pulled him well ahead of Gnaeus whose swimming skills were in need of some refinement. As Timon turned to shout encouragement, he caught sight of a figure waving from the shore. "Someone is calling to us. Can you make out who it is?" he asked Gnaeus.

"It looks like old Marcos, my father's scribe. I guess we better go in and find out what he wants."

Long, full strokes and the incoming tide quickly brought them to the shore where the old scribe, robes flapping in the wind continued shouting his message. "Your father must talk to Timon immediately. He awaits you at the house. Quickly now, don't keep the Honorable Publius waiting."

As they made their way along the path to the estate, anxiety gnawed at Timon. Why had he been summoned? Something important was happening or Publius would never have sent his scribe to find them. It was a long walk from the top of the escarpment down to the sea. Marcos led him through the courtyard into Publius' office. The governor was waiting at his desk.

When Timon entered Publius stood. Greeting him with the traditional Roman salute, he then stepped from behind his desk and embraced him as a brother. "It's good to see you. Is that young son of mine keeping up with his studies? I have never known him to be so excited about learning. He greatly admires you."

"Gnaeus is a fine student with a quick mind and wit. He is excellent in mathematics. He finds languages a challenge, but he is determined to learn."

"I am pleased with that report. But I didn't call you here to check up on my son. I have some concerns about you, especially in view of the news just brought to me from the harbor. Another Alexandrian ship, the Castor and Pollux, has arrived. The captain is preparing to depart for Italy within the week. I can no longer delay a decision regarding your status. Already Cassius has petitioned me to release you to him as his prisoner. He wants to return you to Myra rather than go on to Rome. With the weather improving, there will soon be empty grain ships calling here on their way back to Egypt. He will seek passage on one of them, I am sure."

Old fears knotted in Timon's stomach. "I beseech you, Honorable Publius, do not release me to Cassius. If you do, he will kill me before we are out of sight of this island."

"Timon, talk to me as you would to your father, not as an official of government. As a brother in the Lord, help me to understand your situation so I can make a right decision. Why would Cassius want you dead? You are valuable to him. He says there is a large reward for your capture and return."

"Cassius lies. My master, Marcellos, may have offered some small reward for my return, but he has many slaves, and I am of no special value to him. I am sure there is a reward, but it is for the great pearls that were stolen, stolen by Cassius and blamed on me."

"Pearls? I don't understand."

Timon recounted the events that had led him aboard the Aries and ultimately to the island. As he spoke, his voice grew barbed with anger.

"Timon, I believe what you have said, but that does not change either of our positions under the law. You admit to being a runaway slave. You are still the legal property of Marcellos. I am obligated, under law, to return you to your owner. However, since Cassius does not have legal papers commissioning him to return you as a runaway, I do not have to send you back with him. From what you have said, I have little doubt he will do everything he can to prevent you from reaching Myra. You pose a threat to him and his position with Marcellos. You could expose him as the true thief. I suspect what he really wants is the pearls. If he gets them, your life is forfeit." Publius began to pace, his forehead wrinkled in deep thought. At last he spoke. "I have an idea, but you must trust me. As a government official, I can send an official courier to Marcellos. Do you have the pearls?"

"Yes and no"

"That's no answer. Either you trust me or you don't. You must decide. I'm trying to help you."

"I do trust you, Publius. You misunderstand. I do not have the pearls. I have hidden them. They are aboard the wreck of the..."

Publius suddenly clapped his hand over Timon's mouth, demanding silence. Outside the door the unmistakable sound of flapping sandals on running feet echoed in the courtyard.

Timon paced the length of his quarters trying to honor Publius' request that he stay safely out of sight inside the estate until some decision could be made regarding his future. Impatience and growing fear gnawed at him, grating on his nerves like the sound of stone sharpening a blade. By mid-afternoon he had rehearsed each word of his conversation with Publius and could recite the scene like an actor in a Greek tragedy. He had no doubt as to the identity of the stealthy listener at the door.

"Cassius." He said aloud through barred teeth. "And now he has a good idea where the pearls are hidden. It's just a matter of time before he finds them.. Then he'll come after me." Timon's instincts screamed for action, but his reasoning restrained him from racing to the ship to retrieve the pearls. "Even if I give the pearls to Publius to be returned to Marcellos, the debt is only partly paid. I am the other part. I belong to him as surely as the pearls. I must be returned as well," he reasoned.

Timon hesitated a moment, body arguing with mind, then he turned and walked purposefully from the great house. Turning his back to the sea below he began a slow steady run along the track worn deep by cart ruts. It led toward the capital five miles inland from the estate.

As he reached the edge of the city, perspiration ran in rivulets down the corded muscle channels of his back and legs. Tingling with fatigue, he slowed to a steady walk. Though he had never been in the city before, he moved with confidence, knowing the form it had taken under more than two hundred years of Roman influence.

When he reached its central plaza he searched for a cluster of people that would mark the location he sought.

In the shadow of a building, shielded from the late afternoon sun, he saw Paul. He was deeply involved in animated conversation. Beside him sat Heru, translating both sides of the discussion.

"You see, Christ loves you and gave himself to die for you that you might have everlasting life. It doesn't matter what you are, whether slave or free, Greek, Roman, or foreigner, when you believe and obey my Lord Jesus. You then become citizens of His kingdom and members of the family of God."

A bearded elder stood and addressed Paul, awe and respect in his voice. Heru translated. "We would learn more of this Jesus, honorable prophet. Will you come again tomorrow so we can bring our friends and family to hear your teachings?"

"My time grows short. I must soon travel to Rome to testify of Christ before Caesar." The crowd murmured in wonder at the thought of standing before Rome's ruler. "But be aware, there are already those of 'The Way' living here on the Island. They follow and share the teachings of Jesus. They meet to worship each first day of the week at the estate of Publius, your governor. As for tomorrow, I will be here if it is God's will." With that, he bowed in prayer and dismissed the crowd.

Heru ran forward to embrace his friend. "What brings you to the capital, Timon? Has Publius made you his messenger?"

"No, my friend, I have come to find Paul."

"How can I help you, my son? This must be a matter of some importance to bring you all the way from the estate this late in the day."

Timon reviewed the day's events and the dilemma facing him. Paul listened without comment. "It all looks so hopeless. No matter what I do, I still end up a slave. Even if the pearls are returned, I must return to Marcellos. If Cassius can find the pearls, he will simply disappear."

"No, Timon. I don't think so. Heru injected. There is too much at stake for him to do that. He values his Roman citizenship. If he does not return to Marcellos, he will be a suspect and a fugitive. He won't accept that as a way of life."

"Heru is right, Timon" Paul agreed. "There have to be other solutions. I am sure you have prayed for help in this. I urge you to continue to pray, not simply for a solution but for strength and guidance. Remember, the Lord works for the good of those who love Him."

Timon's clinched his fist as he spoke. "I have trouble with that. I accept that I am the legal property of Marcellos and must return to him. But is it to my good to remain a slave? I don't see it that way. There is nothing fair or just in what has happened to me."

"Patience, my son. God often uses our circumstances to refine us and make us of greater use to him. Think of your own situation. Because of it you have learned of Christ and become His follower. You don't know what our Lord may have in mind for you. For now, you must do what you know is right and trust the outcome to our God. I have arranged with Julius to remain in the city overnight, but I will speak with Publius tomorrow. In the meantime, I will keep you in my prayers."

It was almost sunset when Timon left the city. As he jogged along the path back to the estate, a sense of peace settled over him. Though Paul had given him no solution, he had given him hope and strengthened his faith.

The land rose steadily from the central plain where the city was located. The northern end of the island rose to a high plateau where the estate of Publius sat overlooking the sea. Midway between the city and the estate, a small stream flowing down from the plateau carved a narrow valley. After winding its way to a crossing of the stream, the rutted road again snaked its way up to the opposite side and back out onto the upward sloping land. As sunset faded into darkening shadows, a full moon began to rise.

"I should have left word with someone that I would be late. I may miss the evening meal," Timon thought to himself. As he entered the shadows of the valley, the sense of peace he had taken with him from the city began to dissipate, replaced by a prickly feeling creeping along his back and neck. He searched the deep shadows along the roadway, feeling, but not seeing another living presence nearby.

Chapter 11

Throbbing pain crept relentlessly under the edges of the blanket of blackness wrapping Timon's mind. A low moaning sound penetrated his consciousness as he became aware of his own voice. He struggled to orient himself to his surroundings and realized he was lying face down in the sand. Beyond, he heard the hiss of waves skittering onto the beach. Rough sandals slid under his waist rolling him onto his back as a vortex of nausea swirled around him. It slowly cleared, and he became aware of his hands beneath him, bound behind his back. Above him in the bright moonlight towered the dark form of Cassius.

"About time you woke up, slave boy. I didn't hit you that hard. We've got some things to discuss. To begin with, where are the pearls?"

"I don't have…" Timon gasped as Cassius' foot crashed into his ribs.

"I didn't ask you if you had them. I asked you where they are. I know you've hidden them. I heard that much this afternoon. Now, let's try this again. Where, exactly, are the pearls?"

"Where you'll never find them." A cry of agony escaped Timon's clinched jaws as Cassius kicked him again.

"You don't seem to understand, boy. I want to know exactly where you've hidden the pearls." Cassius voice was oily with sarcasm.

"No. It's you who doesn't understand." Timon's rage overcame his fear and pain. "There's no way you can get them even if I tell you exactly where they are. Face it. I am the only hope you have of ever getting your hands on those pearls. If you keep kicking my ribs, I won't be in any condition to get them either."

"Perhaps you are right, slave boy. But there are ways to make you talk without doing further damage to your body." Cassius grabbed Timon's hair and yanked him upright. "Get moving."

Pushing and shoving Timon ahead of him, they made their way along the rocky course of the stream back up the narrow valley. They left the stream bed and followed an ancient trail broken here and there by rock slides. Clambering over boulders with thorny shrubs tearing at their legs, they followed the trail as it lead upward along the craggy limestone outcropping. Ahead, Timon realized, were the caves of the dead. The trail ended abruptly at a low yawning entrance.

"Why have you brought me here? This won't get the pearls for you."

"Oh, I think it will. This seems like a nice quiet place for you to do some serious thinking. Perhaps we might even reach an agreement of some kind. Think about it."

"I'll never tell you what you want to know. I'd rather die first."

"That's your choice, of course…and if you are going to die, this is a good place to do it. But think it over. If you don't tell me where the pearls are, I can simply leave you here neatly tied and staked. The rats would soon find you. I will take the next ship that sails for Alexandria or Rome, no worse off than before. However, I don't think you will choose to die. It would be a foolish waste. We might even work out a compromise to benefit both of us."

"What are you talking about? I'll never make a bargain with you."

"Oh, but you have yet to consider the possibilities, my young friend. There are several. For one, you could agree to be my partner. If you retrieve the pearls we could leave the island together, sail to Syracuse, Rhegium, Rome or even Alexandria. We could sell the pearls and share the wealth."

"I'm no fool, Cassius. I would be dead before a ship could leave the harbor."

"No, young Timon, you are not a fool, and neither am I. The price of the pearls will not last forever. There will be a continuing need for money. You have special knowledge and a special talent. You inspire trust and confidence. In just three months, look what you have accomplished here. You've been accepted into the house of Publius as one of the family, the trusted tutor. Consider my skills as a thief, young Greek. I stole the best guarded and most valuable treasure of the house of Marcellos from beneath his very nose."

"Yes, you stole those pearls. You could steal others. What makes these so valuable?"

"Ah, you are beginning to understand. Perhaps you have heard the name Aulus Vitalius?"

"Yes. Marcellos mentioned that the emperor appointed him Proconsul of Africa. What does he have to do with this?"

"Everything, in fact. The pearls I stole are a pair. Vitalius commissioned Marcellos to make into earrings as a gift for his mother. Marcellos will not only suffer the loss of the pearls but a loss of reputation with a high Roman official."

"You admit being the thief and yet you nearly killed me with the whip, knowing full well I was not guilty. And you expect me to trust you now?"

"Killing you was my intention, but Marcellos intervened. Now there are other options. There are many treasures in the home of Publius. With your access to that household and my skills, we can greatly enrich ourselves before we move on to Rome. I understand that Greek tutors are much in demand in all the better households. The possibilities are limitless."

"You scum. Do you really think I would stoop to that?"

"One never knows what one might do until opportunities present themselves. But then, your Greek pride was always your downfall. But you've not considered your final option, slave boy." Cassius' voice was as edged as sharpened metal. "You may be willing to sacrifice your own life for your secret, but are you ready to let others die for it?

The question sent a coldness creeping up Timon's spine. "What are you talking about?"

"You're about to have company. While you've been winning the trust of Publius, I have been winning the trust of household slaves. You're not the only one with access to the estate. I come and go as I choose. I happen to know that young Celia is an early riser who often walks alone in the garden just before daylight. I have not been blind to your growing interest in her. It will be a simple matter to bring her here to share your fate."

Blinding rage swept over Timon. He hurled himself at the shadowy form of Cassius as he struggled against his bound hands. With surprising agility the big man side stepped the attack. Lashing out with his foot, he kicked Timon's feet from under him sending him sprawling headlong into the rock floor of the cave.

When consciousness returned, Timon was alone on the cave floor, hands and feet bound together with rawhide thongs. Agony throbbed through his bruised shoulder and head with every heartbeat. Biting his lips, he tried to push the pain from him. As dark waves of despair threatened, Timon began to pray.

Remembering the words of Paul, he began, "Oh Father in heaven, help me. Protect me from this evil man. Release me from my bonds so I can..." He stopped, aware that he was about to ask God's help to destroy Cassius. How could he ask that of a God who taught you to love your enemies? "I hate him. I'll kill him. I want him dead." Bitterness and doubt burned in the tears that rose unbidden to his eyes.

"All things work together for good to those who love God. Trust Him." Those were Paul's words. "Sure they have, Paul. This is just what I needed. Is this God's way of rewarding those who try to follow Him?" Slowly anger and desire for revenge replaced despair. As cold, calculating reason returned, Timon began to plan, mentally weighing hard realities against possibilities. He had only one weapon - Cassius' fear of water.

Chapter 12

The first rays of morning had begun to light the cave entrance when Timon heard the scrape of footsteps on the rocky escarpment outside. Moments later a small shadow entered haltingly followed by the unmistakable form of Cassius.

Timon gasped as Cassius again kicked him in his ribs. "Good morning slave boy. I told you I'd bring you some company. I always keep my word. I believe you know this young lady. She has agreed, somewhat reluctantly, to guarantee your cooperation."

"You're a fool, Cassius. Now you will never get off this island alive."

"Oh, but I will boy, and so will you if you are as smart as I think you are. Listen carefully. One of the empty grain ships sails for Alexandria on the tide, just about mid-day. I will agree to leave the lovely Celia unharmed in the cave here. You can send a courier to Publius telling him where to find her. Of course, that's after you have delivered the pearls to me and I am safely at sea. If not, I'll leave you both here to join the other residents of the Caves of the Dead. Now, where are the pearls? You are already pretty well banged up. Don't tempt me to break your arms and legs as well."

Across the small fire Cassius had lighted, Timon read the unmistakable message Celia was sending. Her eyes looking out at him above the cloth that wrapped her mouth were wide with terror, but she shook her head in an emphatic "No."

I'm sorry Celia. I have no choice. He will kill both of us if I don't tell him. You win, Cassius. I will tell you. Then we'll see if you have the guts to claim them."

"You'd better explain yourself, boy. Time is running out and so is my patience. Where are the pearls?"

"Aboard the wreck of the Aries."

Uncertainty flashed across Cassius' face. "You lie. There's nothing left aboard that hulk. Quit stalling."

"I'm telling you the truth. Remember the day you found me below deck with one of Luke's scalpels? I used that blade to carve a hole at the base of the mast where it is connected to the cross braces. I put the pearls inside and covered the hole with pitch. They are out there in what is left of the wreck buried below twelve feet of water. I don't think you have the guts to retrieve them. I remember your panic when the Aries sank. You don't know how to swim."

Cassius' fist slammed into Timon's face and he spat blood from his mouth. In spite of the pain, he smiled in satisfaction. He had touched a raw nerve in his captor. Clearly shaken by this unexpected development, Cassius said nothing for a moment. Then he rose and strode out of the cave.

When he returned he was carrying a coil of braided rope. Timon recognized it as the kind local fishermen used to give shape to their casting nets. Cassius roughly ran the rope behind Timon's neck and under his arms forming a harness. He yanked the rope tight and knotted it between Timon's aching shoulder blades. Without speaking, he untied the leather thongs binding Timon's feet and wrists. Then he sneered, "You're going to swim, slave boy, and for her sake, you'd better not try to slip out of this harness."

Leaving Celia bound and on the cave floor, Cassius shoved Timon through the cave opening and down the winding trail ahead of him. When they reached the bay,

Timon could see the up-turned hull of a small fishing boat which Cassius must have used to bring Celia to the cave. Beyond was the jagged mast of the wreck, pointing at an angle toward the rising sun.

"Take off your toga and give it to me." As Timon handed him his outer garment, Cassius uncoiled another rope and knotted it to the harness binding his shoulders. "Just so you don't try to swim away once you have the pearls."

"I'll need your help down there. I can't do this alone with this rope weighing me down. Besides, I'll need a knife to dig out the pearls. You'll have to come with me."

"Oh, I think you'll manage. Just consider what will happen if you fail. Pick up that flat rock. You can scrape pitch with that."

Cassius dragged the boat into the water, and with a shove motioned Timon to get aboard. The boat knifed through the water, responding to the powerful pull Cassius applied to the oars. They were about five hundred yards from the wreck when Timon began to feel the drag of the cross current that swept around the shoals where the ship ran aground. Cassius struggled to steer the boat across the rip tide into deeper water beyond. At last he managed to maneuver the boat alongside the tilting hulk rocking gently on the incoming tide.

"Do it!" Cassius barked when he had secured the boat to the wreck. "And remember, if you don't come back, she dies."

Timon slid into the water and began to swim along the water soaked planking, his battered body paying in agony for each stroke. To reach the base of the mast, he would have to find a way inside the hull. He dived deeper feeling the increasing weight of the wet harness rasping his shoulders, neck and back. He felt his way along the rough planking. Suddenly there was only water. A gaping hole opened into the body of the dead ship.

Inside, between the water level and the wreck above, he knew he would find an air space where he could recharge his starved lungs. He burst to the surface gasping. "I'll have to start from here. The rope is too short. Bring the boat closer."

"Cassius hesitated, then moved the boat into the shadow of the wreck. "Get on with it. We don't have much time left."

Timon dived again, pushing himself through the torn planking and into the dark interior. He broke surface inside the hull. He took a deep breath of dank air and began groping in the darkness for the cylindrical form of the mast. The darkness seemed to move in on him. Closing his eyes tightly, he recalled the angle of the mast outside trying to visualize his position in relation to it. As he opened his eyes and peered into the darkness, claustrophobia and panic clawed at his mind.

Then a small patch, not of light, but of lesser darkness appeared, marking his entry point. Focus returned. In a few strokes he felt the rounded, slimy form of the main mast angling into the uplifted under decking six feet below him. He filled his lungs again and began pulling himself downward, feeling his way along the great timber until he felt the place where the mast attached to the hull of the ship. Stretching his fingers, he searched for the ring bolt he had used for a marker. Probing like a blind man, he felt for the raised surface which marked the spot where he had applied a thick coating of pitch. Using the rock, he scraped away the slime coating the great timber, until he at last could feel the raised smoothness of the coating of pitch. His lungs were screaming for air. Using the mast as a guide, he allowed the buoyancy of his body to bring him back to the airspace below the deck.

Suddenly, waves of red agony racked his body as Cassius yanked the cord binding them together. Timon retched into the sea as the rope tore at his bruised shoulder. He burst through the opening in the deck and surfaced beside the boat shaking his fist and screaming at Cassius.

"Are you insane? I have enough to deal with down in that hole without having to deal with your stupidity. Make up your mind. Either let me do what you sent me to do or kill me and get it over with. Right now, I don't much care which you choose."

Cassius drew back in surprise from the cauldron of rage he had pulled from beneath the deck.

"You'd been down a long time. I was afraid you'd escaped or drowned."

"You are nothing but a coward. Only a coward would act like you do. You're even afraid of a little water. I've found where the pearls are hidden, but I can't get them out without a knife. Now, either give me the knife, unless you're afraid of a man with only one good arm. Or get down here and help me."

"I'll...I'll come with you." Cassius knotted the cord around his waist and slid tentatively into the water. As Timon dived, he realized the morning sun was brightening the water. He disappeared into the hole below deck.

Inside, Timon glanced over his shoulder to watch as Cassius squeezed himself into the cavern. Even in the dim light, he could see panic creeping across the big man's face.

In the air space Cassius caught his breath. Between gasps he said, "Wait for me now. How far do we have to go?"

"Timon pointed to the tilting mast timber overhead. "It's at the base of the mast, about eight feet below. There are some loose braces where the mast was fastened to the hull. The pearls are just below them. Come on."

As Timon took a deep breath to dive, he heard the timbers of the wreck groan as if squeezed by a giant hand. He hesitated only a moment, realizing the hulk was shifting in the tide. Then he dived. Light had begun to penetrate the deeper water, and he could see the bulging frightened face of Cassius moving toward him clutching the tether like a lifeline. Timon gestured toward the blackened splotch on the mast, motioning to Cassius to begin digging away the pitch. After two or three thrusts with the blade, Cassius pointed upward. Timon followed him.

"You're wasting your air," Timon gasped at him. "Make every movement count. Breathe out in small bursts."

Cassius only nodded and followed Timon back into the depths. They made two more trips to the surface, but on the third dive, the blade slid through the pitch, and a small bubble burst out. They had found the pearls.

In his excitement, Cassius thrust the blade into the mast and began to probe the carved hole, searching for the silky smoothness of the pearls. Retrieving them, he carefully placed them in the bag he carried at his waist. As Cassius grasped the knife still protruding from the mast, Timon read his murderous intent.

Grabbing the braided tether with his good arm, Timon jerked the line. The sudden tension tore Cassius tentative grip from the mast. Timon dived beneath a broken timber wedged against the mast. Using the beam for leverage, he braced his feet and pulled slowly dragging the terrified man deeper toward the maze of wreckage at the bottom of the ship. Cassius frantically slashed at the braided cord as he tried to resist the relentless downward pull. As Timon pulled, the braids of the rope began to separate. Cassius' head and shoulders were under the timber when the blade bit into the rope severing it. The sudden change in pressure had loosened the huge broken beam. Timon watched in fascination. Slowly, it shifted positions driving its jagged end into Cassius' shoulder and pinning him to the mud and slime of the sunken deck.

Released from the tether and with his lungs screaming for air, Timon propelled himself into the airspace overhead. Sucking great draughts of the damp air into his body, he felt a thrill of exultation. Cassius was trapped and would soon be dead.

"At last. I have longed for his death, and now it's inevitable." Timon wondered for a moment if he could have plunged the knife into the man. He rejoiced with relief in the knowledge that it was the sea and Cassius' own greed that even now was killing the Roman. "As a Christian I could not have killed him. Now he will die, and I'll not be guilty of his blood."

The words were like a blow across his consciousness. Images of a Roman courtroom and an indifferent governor flashed through his mind...Pontius Pilate, a man with the power of life and death, a guilty man who sanctioned death because he chose to do nothing.

Even as Timon was mentally justifying his reasons, his slender form plunged again into the wreckage below him. A new panic, born of the pressure of time, gnawed at his resolve. He stopped briefly to twist a small wooden brace from its anchor on the side of a collapsed bulkhead before continuing his frantic dive.

Fighting the current, he used his hip and good arm to maneuver one end of the small timber under the beam which pinned Cassius to the deck. Using one of the deck ribs as a fulcrum, Timon threw his body weight onto the lever. Slowly, the great beam shuddered. Groaning under the opposing pressure, it began to move.

It was enough to release Cassius from its grip. Below him, Timon could see the unconscious, oxygen starved face of his enemy, his useless outstretched hand still clutching the knife.

Time and hope were running out. Timon released the pressure on the beam and dived. In a deft motion he grabbed the knife and severed the rope that had once bound him to Cassius. Thrusting with his feet, he fought his way back to the lever. Applying as much weight as his own buoyancy would allow, he leaned into the beam. It was enough. Again the beam released Cassius as Timon began reeling in the tether. As Cassius' body moved out of the trap, redness blossomed around his shoulder. Timon thrust himself forward, pulling the inert body after him. Desperately, he fought his way to the surface, his lungs again screaming for air. Even as he struggled to the surface, he sensed a change in the water currents. Eddys of bottom mud swirled around him. Creaks and groans from stressed ship timbers echoed eerily through the water. Cross currents tugged at Cassius' lifeless form bringing a stab of agony to Timon's bruised shoulder. A storm was rising.

As his head broke through the surface, Timon had only time for a quick gasp of air before being buried again by a wave breaking over him. Frantically, he fought his way through tons of gray-green sea and clawed upward toward the leaping boat tethered to the moaning wreck. With his last ounces of strength, he heaved Cassius' arms and shoulders over the edge of the boat. Bright swirls of light floated across encroaching blackness as he teetered on the edge of exhaustion.

"No. If I pass out we'll both die here." More from strength of will than strength of body, he drew himself back from the abyss. With Cassius between him and the gunwale of the boat, he thrust his shoulder into the Roman's back. Again and again he slammed into the inert form until at last he heard the retching gasp he had been hoping for as Cassius emptied ingested sea water into the boat and sucked life giving air into empty lungs.

Though Cassius was breathing again, consciousness did not return. He hung, suspended by his arms, over the side of the boat, still floating in a coma on a storm-stirred sea. Timon grasped the side of the tossing boat, and using his own body to keep Cassius from being pitched back into the sea, he grimly assessed his situation. Cassius outweighed him by at least fifty pounds. There was no way he could hoist the man's unconscious body into the boat.

Perhaps I could tie him to the boat and swim to shore for help, he reasoned, remembering the day of the shipwreck when the sea was full of floating debris and frightened sailors. But there was no floating debris in the water now. A wave lifted him. He measured the distance to the shore against his own depleted strength and shook his head in despair. It was too far.

"You may cost me my life, yet." he said aloud. He felt the regular rhythm of the Roman's breathing replace his ragged gasping. "I was stupid to try to save you. If you were conscious, the only thanks I'd get would be a knife in the chest"

Black rage rose again in Timon's mind as he remembered all the evil this man had done to him. A bright spark of temptation flickered, threatening to burst into flame. "All I have to do is turn you loose. The sea will do the rest. Then I can get into the boat and make it to shore. No one can blame me. Celia heard your threats. She knows what you had planned for us. Besides, if I stay here with you, we may both drown, and that will mean Celia dies as well. Why should I die for such as you?"

His own words caught and held him. Paul's strong voice echoed through Timon's mind. "In this way God demonstrates how much he loves each of us. While we were still sinners, Christ died for us." Mentally, Timon finished the argument. The flame of rage and temptation was extinguished, as if by one of the waves that now threatened him. A strange sense of compassion filled him as he held the body of the helpless man against the boat. With it came the weight of awareness. He held the man's life in his hands."

A sudden tautness jerked the tether holding the boat to the mast. Above the hiss of wave and wind he again heard the grinding groan of shifting, collapsing timbers.

The stub of the mast lifted a few feet, titled toward the sea and plunged beneath the swirling waves as the hulk, loosened from its entrapment in bay mud, rolled onto its side and was swept into deep water by the undercurrents of the bay. The small boat, suddenly upended, flipped Cassius and Timon, along with its contents into the water. The boat, still tethered to the wreck, disappeared into the great maw of the sea. Timon fought against the yawning vortex which swirled around him, threatening to swallow both him and his burden. In a digestive belch, the sea spewed out the boat's captive air. Like a nauseated beast, it began disgorging loosened debris from the sunken ship's belly along with a few broken timbers and braces, all that remained to mark the ships ultimate grave.

A few determined strokes brought Timon within reach of a curved piece of wood, part of one of the curved braces from the ship's upper hold. He grasped the fragment and tied Cassius to it with the strand of rope that had once tethered him to his enemy. Rolling onto his back, towing Cassius behind him he began a one-armed struggle toward the shore. Timon prayed. "I have done what I can, Father. The rest is up to you."

Time was lost in surging seas and the endless agony of stroke after stroke of an aching arm. Some time after he had felt the abrasive scrape of sand and shells against his back, he became aware of nearby shouting and the grip of strong hands dragging him from the surf. He awoke to the warmth and the crackling of a fire. He opened his eyes to see the anxious face of Heru, hovering over him.

"He's waking up. He's going to make it."

"Give him a few sips of this." Luke's finely featured face came into focus as he gently lifted Timon to swallow the herbal broth.

Between coughs and gasps for breath, Timon tried to form his questions but Luke quieted him.

Cassius is here Timon, thanks to you. But he's more dead than alive. What happened?"

As the bitter broth slowly warmed him, Timon's awareness returned. "Never mind that now. You have to find Celia."

"Where is she? She's the one we were looking for when we found you floundering in the waves on the beach. Publius has half the island out looking for her."

"Cassius kidnapped her and took her to the Caves of the Dead. She's tied up in one of them."

"Don't worry. We'll find her," Heru assured him. Luke will stay here with you until you're stronger. I'll send help to get you back to the estate."

With that, Heru was gone and Timon slipped into a peaceful sleep, his responsibilities handed to others.

When he awoke he was in his own quarters at the estate. The pungent odor of burning olive oil and the flickering shadows told him it was evening. A gentle hand touched his shoulder as he tried to sit up. "Rest easy, my son. You've had quite a day, I understand. But God has been good, and all is well. You've been in our prayers and we will continue to pray for Cassius. He still lingers between life and death.

"I am glad you are here, Paul, but I thought you were to sail for Rome this afternoon."

"That was the plan, but the storm you hear outside still rages. The captain of the Castor and Pollux refused to sail until the weather settles again."

"I'm thankful for that. There are things I need to say to you, things I don't understand. Besides, I would not have wanted you to sail without a chance to bid you God's blessings."

"I'm also glad of the delay though I am eager to get to Rome. I did not want to sail without giving you instructions for continuing the work of the Lord in this place."

"You sound as if I will be staying here. How can that be? You know I am a runaway slave. That makes me a fugitive from Roman law. Won't Julius take me on to Rome as a prisoner?"

You may some day see Rome, my son, but I do not believe it will be soon. The Lord is sending me to be His witness in Rome. I have prayed long about the infant church that has begun to grow here. I believe the Lord has a mission for you in this place."

"That's impossible, isn't it? If I stay here after you leave for Rome, that will make Publius guilty of sheltering a fugitive. He could loose his office and have his estates stripped from him. He could even be arrested. Besides, after today, I am not sure I am fit to serve the Lord anywhere."

"One thing at a time, Timon. First, the decision as to whether or where you go is out of your hands. Others will make that choice. I have prayed for their guidance in this. It is in God's hands. Have no doubt He saved us from the sea for His own purposes. Know that you are in His care. But tell me why you feel unfit to serve Our Lord. Celia has already told us of Cassius' plan and her kidnapping. I understand the pearls were still aboard the wreck of the Aires. What happened out there?"

Slowly, and in every detail, Timon retold the story. Paul intently listened as Timon recounted his experience. "When I saw Cassius trapped down there I wanted him dead. I tried to leave him there, but I couldn't. I wanted to let him drown.

"But you didn't. The Lord gave you strength. You let the Spirit of the Lord guide you. Otherwise, Cassius would be dead."

"Just the same, I wanted him dead. I hated him. I was too weak to kill him, but I wanted him dead."

"Listen to me. The key to understanding is in what you just said. It is when we are weak that we discover our true strength. Only after we have emptied ourselves do we have room for the power of the Lord in our lives. Cassius lives. He's in the room next door. Luke is attending him. You saved his life. How do you feel about him now, and how will you feel when he regains his hold on life?"

"I don't really know. I don't have the energy to hate him. I know he is my enemy, but I hope he lives."

Paul smiled with affection and pride. "Yes, perhaps he is your enemy, but you were willing to risk your life for him. Jesus told us there are few who would do that for a friend, much less for an enemy. Will you pray with me for his recovery?"

After three days, the late winter storm had spent its furry. Now a feeble sun filtered through the atrium outside Publius' study.

"So what's to be done with you, my brother?" Publius smiled as he searched Timon's face. "Cassius will recover, but I daresay, he will never be quite the same man as the one you rescued from the wreck."

Responding to Timon's questioning look, Publius continued. "Oh, he will regain his health. But you have confused him thoroughly. The pearls are safely in my care and will be returned to Marcellos in due course along with a full accounting of this adventure. Your friend Heru tells me that Cassius wants you to explain what made you want to save his life."

"Perhaps I will have time to explain it to him on our trip back to Myra. I must go back with him. I still belong to Marcellos, just as the pearls do. Both properties must be returned to their rightful owner." An edge of bitterness crept into Timon's studied response.

A smile flickered at the corners of Publius' mouth as he spoke. "You may consider yourself as property if you wish. I do not. But since you do, has it occurred to you that property can be both bought and sold."

Julius' hearty laughter rumbled through the room, further adding to the confusion Timon felt. "It seems that Cassius is not the only one with questions, young Greek. Perhaps it is time for explanations. The Honorable Publius and I have had many discussions while you were away. Though Cassius is improving, he would not be able to travel, even if a ship were available. Then there is the matter of his status before the law. He now admits to the theft of the pearls. We have his confession, but no charge. That is a matter to be resolved in Myra, not in Rome. He also admits to kidnapping Celia. That is a matter of local jurisdiction and must be handled by the chief magistrate of Malta, the Honorable Publius. He is more inclined to mercy and forgiveness than to prosecution. There is no understanding you Christians."

"Then am I to go to Rome with you?" Timon asked.

With a sweeping gesture, Julius referred the question to the smiling Publius. "This is where the matter of buying and selling property is of interest. I do not know the sale price of a runaway slave in Myra, but it should not be too great for my resources. Paul carries with him to the agents of Marcellos in Rome, my offer to pay his asking price. Since he also carries the pearls and Cassius' signed confession of the theft, I have no doubt that he will accept my offer. When the transaction is complete you will be, not only my brother in Christ, but my fellow laborer with the church here on Malta. You will be free.

With the twin figureheads of Castor and Pollux facing into the crisp golden morning, the great ship turned its bow toward Rome. Timon thought of Paul and Luke as he swallowed the emotional knot in his throat. Then he spoke. "Those two great men will change the Roman Empire."

"And these two great men," said Celia, clasping the hands of Publius and Timon, "will change our world on Malta."